BY HIS SIDE

To Theresa & Serge,
With many fond
memories.

Jimmy Berton

FOUNTAIN SQUARE
PUBLISHING LLC

Library of Congress Control Number: 2020910056
ISBN-13: 978-0-9724421-4-5

Page design: Chad DeBoard
Cover design: Chad DeBoard
Production Assistance: Robert Flischel

Printed in Canada.
First American Edition, 2020

Fountain Square Publishing LLC: Cincinnati

www.fountainsquarepublishing.com

For all those who bore the chains of slavery and for
those who helped break those chains.

For my family whose support and assistance helped
an idea become a book.

OTHER WORKS BY
JINNY POWERS BERTEN

Littsie of Cincinnati
 With Norah Holt

Littsie and the Underground Railroad

Jake and Sam at the Empty Abbey

Henri: A Christmas Donkey Story

Cincinnati Christmas

We Dance

BY HIS SIDE

THE STORY OF
GEORGE WASHINGTON
AND WILLIAM LEE

A Work of Historical Fiction by
Jinny Powers Berten

CONTENTS

Chapter 1: Memories   1

Chapter 2: William Lee   19

Chapter 3: Table Talk   30

Chapter 4: Other Observations   42

Chapter 5: A Star-Filled Night   52

Chapter 6: Stones in My Heart   65

Chapter 7: Grave Concerns   69

Chapter 8: The Salute   81

Chapter 9: 'Tis Well   86

Chapter 10: Keeping Watch   90

Chapter 11: Facing Death's Reality   94

Chapter 12: Getting Ready   99

Chapter 13: Right By His Side   103

Chapter 14: Time to Say Goodbye   107

Chapter 15: A Questionable Future   111

Chapter 16: Work to Be Done   115

Chapter 17: Fulfilling Wishes   117

Chapter 18: Aftermath   149

Chapter 19: Plots, Fears, and Early Freedom   153

Chapter 20: Free At Last   157

Acknowledgments   X

Illustration Credits   163

Bibliography   164

Author's Note   168

ACKNOWLEDGMENTS

Many people help make words find their way into a book and I have many to thank.

The staff at Mount Vernon was extremely helpful and knowledgeable. From our first meeting at the library, Mary Thompson has shared her amazing store of knowledge concerning all things Mount Vernon. Dawn Bonner gave direction and suggestions that helped make the photo illustrations work well. Her deep knowledge of the photo collections led us down the right path. Her patience with questions and suggestions solved many problems. Thank you Dawn.

Kyra Swanson at Washington and Lee University provided information concerning the Washington family tree. Thank you.

Georgia J Brown at the Fairfax County Historical Records Center, Fairfax Circuit Court, knows everything about George Washington's will and supplied accurate pictures from the original. Thank you, Georgia.

Many thanks to Ken Schuermann, who once again gave good advice on the ways of horses. And thanks to Dr. Liz Brown, as well, who taught me the difference between a hound and a dog.

Thanks also to Dr. John Shockley, who explained George Washington's illness, epiglottitis, its causes and effects, as well as how it was treated in the eighteenth century.

A special thank-you to Pam Smith, American history teacher at St. Ursula Academy, Cincinnati, who gave valuable insights into the time period and characters.

Anne Montague, the best kind of editor, concise, thorough, diplomatic, and nice to work with, helped in myriad ways.

And the readers, Dr. Liz Brown, John W., Mary Jerome, John, Jane, Shannon, Bonnie, and Pam all gave valuable suggestions and insights.

George Washington

Robert Flischel once again provided his talent with the camera, creating pictures that blend with and add warmth to the story. He brings a sense of humor to his work as well as a love of history.

Ever patient Chad DeBoard, whose imagination and creative talents designed a beautiful book. Thanks so much.

And to my husband, John, who provided advice, insight, time, and suggestions to help create this book, I say thank you many times over

William Lee

Chapter One

MEMORIES

Thursday
December 12, 1799
5 a.m.

Rain fell in spurts on the plantation that sat high above the river. It fell on the stable, the house, the field, the barns, the people, and the animals. The first few days of December 1799 had been mild and cool. Now the weather came as expected, cold and wet.

It was nearing five in the morning. The man stretched his six foot three frame and rolled over, listening to the sounds of the ancient river that flowed only yards from the house. Leaving the mountains behind, the mighty Potomac made its way over falls, through valleys and flatlands, rolling uncontrollably toward the sea.

He was born surrounded by the scent of this water and had lived near it since he was a child. He knew the sounds of the birds nestled in the trees along the shore, the quack of the ducks that paddled into the stream, the croaking of the blue heron, the cawing

William Lee   I

of seagulls, and the high-pitched whistle of the eagle that surveyed the still dark sky. He remembered there had been a large circle around the moon the night before; usually that meant a storm was coming. The Algonquin tribes in the area also believed it forecast personal trouble. Now the weather was cloudy, cold, and wet. The wetness penetrated the house and the cabins and outbuildings on the property. It sat upon the river producing random fog.

George Washington was a man connected to his environment. Growing up, he had been shaped by its challenges and its gifts. Pushed by his mother to tame nature into supporting life's needs, he learned the lesson well. His father's death at forty-nine forced the eleven- year- old's connection to his natural surroundings to grow even more. As the oldest of five siblings, he was schooled in plantation management early and placed in a leadership positions. His determined mother demanded much of her children. Now, ready to rise in the five o'clock winter darkness he remembered his mother's shrill insistence that is when the day begins.

His wife of forty years lay next to him, softly snoring. Martha Dandridge Custis was a widow with two children when they met. She had given birth to four children by her first husband, Daniel Parke Custis. Two died as toddlers, and as a result she had been highly protective of the remaining son and daughter. At five feet, she was much shorter than her six foot three second husband. She was vivacious, charming, steadfast, and gentle throughout their marriage. And he had asked much of her. When he went off to war, he was confident she was capable of running their plantation, Mount Vernon. Organized and disciplined, she had the skills needed to run a vast estate. She was with him through many trials of the war, always aware that Mount Vernon could be burned to the ground and she taken hostage by the British. She visited him at Valley Forge, Cambridge, Philadelphia, and New York. She brought certain calmness to her husband and motherly concern to his soldiers. When he became president of a new country and a new type of government, her support as friend, confidante, and adviser helped define the new land of liberty.

He thought of their joyous wedding day in 1759. He, so handsome in blue velvet, accentuating his blue-gray eyes, she in yellow damask and fashionable shoes from London. The children were dressed in lovely formal wear. The twenty-eight-year-old bride and twenty-seven-year-old groom were both delighted to have found each other. There were many similarities in their backgrounds. Both the oldest of their siblings, George and Martha had assumed leadership in their families. They both attended Church of England services, and neither had received formal schooling. Neither of their families would have been considered part of the aristocracy, but both had found mentors from whom they learned the customs and expectations of that class. Both had been and still were slave owners. They were both hard workers, devout, disciplined and well aware of the needs of a plantation. They enjoyed entertaining and being with other people. And they enjoyed being with each other.

Martha brought not only two children to the marriage but a great deal of money—money that would give George the prestige and privilege he did not have as a child. Interesting, he thought, that both of them were the oldest of their siblings and all of their siblings had died. Only they remained. But the dream had come again last night. It was always the same. He sees his wife, then she fades and he is left alone. What did it mean? he pondered. Would

William Lee 3

he join his siblings soon? Smothering the thought, he rolled over and observed his wife. He would not wake her at this early hour. Her busy day would begin soon enough.

He heard the door softly open. Caroline, who had been up since four, stoked the fire so the room would be warm when her master rose. He heard the fire crackle and smelled the burning wood as it blended with the scent of the river. He waited for the familiar sounds that signaled Caroline had left the room. Slowly he moved the bed curtains, got up and replaced them to keep his wife warm. He relieved himself in the chamber pot that Caroline would empty later. Then he found the basin of warm water she had brought so he could wash. He splashed his face and then wetted a cloth to wash the creases of the body where skin met skin. A full bath would not come until spring. He rinsed out his mouth several times to prevent infection in his gums. Having only one tooth left, he had tried many sets of false teeth but never found anything near to comfortable. Now, remaining in his nightshirt, he lit a candle, found his dressing gown and slippers, and then padded down the back steps to the study below.

He always experienced a brief surge of satisfaction as he entered this room, which he had designed as part of an addition in 1774 as a personal and private space. It had served him well throughout the war and his years as President. It continued to bring him comfort. Caroline would have been busy here as well stoking the fire, lighting candles, cleaning the hearth, opening the curtains, dusting the furniture, and providing hot tea. His enslaved butler, Frank, had brought his favorite hound, Sweetlips, into the study, ready to greet the master when he arrived.

"Good morning, Sweetlips," he said to the hound, patting its

head and giving it a good rub. "Now, you can't make noise. The mistress does not like hounds in the house, but since it is just you and I this morning, she does not have to know. Lie down by the fire. You know, friend, we are both getting old, our joints are creaking, and our ears are not in the best order. I am wearing spectacles. Pity they don't make them for hounds. Quiet, now!"

He began his day with prayer, as was his custom, using a small, well-worn, handwritten prayer book he had carried with him for many, many years.

THURSDAY MORNING PRAYER
Most Gracious Lord God, whose dwelling is in the highest heavens,
and yet behold the lowly and humble upon earth,
I blush and am ashamed to lift up my eyes to Thy dwelling place,
because I have sinned against Thee.
Look down, I beseech Thee, upon me, Thine unworthy servant
Who prostrates myself at the footstool of Thy mercy, confessing my own guiltiness,
and begging pardon for my sins.
What couldst Thou have done, Lord, more for me,
Or what could I have done more against Thee?

Pausing a few moments, he picked up his quill and began answering some of the many letters on his desk. Then he organized the accounts, wrote in his diary, and filed the numerous important papers his daily life produced. His work was detailed, systematic and fastidious.

The breath of dawn crept under the study window, landing on the opposite wall and slowly filling the room with soft light.

Sounds outside brought familiar comfort, often accompanied by suppressed guilt. He could hear the footsteps of the enslaved and the sound of their muffled voices as they prepared to begin their daily routine of unpaid labor on his farms, in the cookhouse, the stables, the barn, the spinning house, the carriage house, the greenhouse, and the house itself. This was not an isolated cabin in the Ohio Country. This was a business supported by 87 enslaved people: 59 adults and 28 children under the age of fourteen. This was a thriving village that produced wheat, corn, vegetables, whiskey, and fish. They wove cloth, made farm tools and horseshoes, tended and cared for sheep, cattle, and horses, landscaped the grounds, sent products to nearby communities and on to Europe. He owned this village and the people who worked there, as well as the 386 human beings who worked on the rest of the thousands of acres that he owned. Slavery had been a natural condition in his life. He had never been without slaves. He had inherited 11 human beings when his father died and continually bought more. Slavery was legal throughout his world and much of the world beyond. And in many places slaves were not considered human. He was the chief executor and manager of slaves, indentured servants and free men who worked on his plantation.

About seven o'clock the great sixty-pound bell rang, signaling that breakfast would soon be served. George made his way to the candlelit, dining room, looking forward to the cornmeal pancakes known as hoecakes—legend had it they could be cooked on a hoe. Lucy, the enslaved cook, would have them ready, hot and drenched in honey, three hoecakes with butter and several dishes of tea, perhaps a few herring. It would be served by her husband, Frank, also a slave. Martha and house guests would join the General.

William Lee

Perhaps one of the visiting children would come to breakfast as well and discuss the day ahead. He loved children and regretted he had none of his own. He had been like a father to his stepchildren, who had both died young: Patsy in 1773 at seventeen and John Parke Custis, known as Jack, in 1781 at twenty-seven. Jack left four children. The two youngest, Eleanor Parke Custis, known as Nelly, two, and Washy, as George Washington Parke Custis was called in childhood, six months, came to the plantation to live with the Washingtons, bringing lightness and gaiety to a house that welcomed them as their own. Now, almost twenty years later, Nelly lay in a bedroom upstairs with her newborn child, Frances Parke Lewis. What a joy to have her child born right here at Mount Vernon.

Each day the General would inspect his wide holdings, five farms and eight thousand acres. Weather never stopped him, and this cold, wet day would be no different. He would normally ride twenty miles inspecting fence building and the condition of winter fields, conferring with the overseers and speaking with his slaves. As a hands-on plantation owner, he did not consider it beneath him to help his employees or even his slaves when he saw a need.

"I will dress now," he announced to his valet, Christopher Sheels, a slave. "Tell Mr. Hardiman to bring my horse around." Christopher followed him to the dressing room off the study.

Here the General shaved himself, then pulled on his cotton stockings, followed by blue overalls. Christopher brushed his gray hair still tinged with the copper red of his youth, pulled it back military style, tied it with a ribbon, fluffed and lightly powdered the side hair. The General inspected his knee-high leather boots, well broken in now to the perfect fit. He turned them round and round to make sure they had been cleaned properly. If they did not meet his expectations, he would throw them at his valet's head without a word. Immediately they would be recleaned. Then Christopher would step forward and help him with his shirt and hold his heavy coat for him.

"It will be a wet one today," said the General, slipping his arms into the sleeves, "but I have seen much worse. I am anxious to get outside."

They opened the front door just as the horse arrived. Steam rose from the animal's massive body and his heavy breath turned to vapor as he met the penetrating cold after the warmth of the stable. He was prancing and snorting, eager to get under way.

Washington gazed at his horse with appreciation. He was an excellent horseman who instinctively understood the animal, its abilities and needs. He looked for well-defined withers, a long neck, deep shoulders, and a strong chest. He wanted his horse to be calm and devoted, yet spirited. With a horse under him he looked at once relaxed, poised, and powerful. Christopher made sure that the food Lucy had prepared and put in the lunch box was secure and then offered him a leg up as he mounted and settled into the familiar saddle. Age had made riding more difficult, but he had faced greater problems. He did not let advancing years slow him down.

He would ride by himself today. He wanted to go toward Dogue Run Farm to inspect cattle pens. He needed to check the condition of the fencing, make sure the corn was being taken to the mill, that the wheat was being cleaned, rye threshed, and carrots dug. Since Christmas was drawing near, he would direct his slaves to cart baby pigs to the house and provide enough wood for the Mansion's

William Lee

many fireplaces. He would remind them that turkeys and chickens would also be needed for the famous Christmas dinner.

A mixture of rain and snow came sluggishly from the west, muddying the roads and falling frozen on the barren fields. It began to roll down the neck of his coat and down his back. He paid no heed to any discomfort. A man of his experience had long ago learned to make peace with weather.

Many memories crowded his brain as he and his horse navigated the snow-clad trail. He thought of his companion and slave William Lee.

"I remember the day I bought him," he mused. "Got him at an auction from the Widow Lee over in Westmoreland County." It was an important auction and drew many people. The slave stock was very valuable. It held much more interest than the animal stock. Slave dealers, farmers, bankers, people who just wanted to own somebody besides themselves were all there. "I bought both William and his younger brother, Frank. I think I paid around a hundred pounds. Mulatto brothers. William must have been about sixteen."

They presented well at the auction, both of them, athletic and strong. William was short and compact, powerfully built. Both were quick and responsive. They had an added value because they were four generations out of Africa. They spoke English well and they understood their place on a plantation. They were there to work. "I was looking for a valet and I thought the boy could do the job. The widow said their mother was a house slave and they were familiar with what was expected in that position. Took them home in a cart that very day."

The General had a lot of ground to cover and rode on now at

a canter, his head lowered against the wet snow. Mount Vernon's holdings ran ten miles along the Potomac and about four miles inland. He had a keen interest in the science of agriculture and always had many projects going at once. He had come to think of himself as a trustee of God's earth. Today he wanted to see how the new superior line of sheep was faring in the winter and check out his gristmill and sixteen-sided barn at Dogue Run Farm. He built the grist mill beside a stream, where refined flour and cornmeal were packed and sent to other parts of the country, even to Portugal. He offered the services of the mill to his neighbors as well. He did not miss a chance to visit his sixteen-sided round barn. Today the visit was even more welcome as the building offered a respite from the cold, wet day. He had built the barn, two stories high with a conical roof, to shelter the horses he put to work threshing his grain. Horses were led to the second floor over an earthen ramp. Grain was laid out on the floor so that the movement of the horses separated the grain from the stalk. Floorboards were laid so that the grain could fall through and be collected. George Washington was proud of his invention. He dismounted and led his horse through the massive, creaking door into the sheltering barn. Light, speckled with dust, penetrated the interior, promising comfort and a dry escape.

The warm building smelled of grain, manure, leather, hay, saddle soap, and wet horses. Tools and horse tack hung neatly on the walls.

"Finally," he thought, "they are treating the equipment properly. Took a while for them to follow orders."

Several horses had found shelter from the weather in the stalls lining the walls. They nickered now, swishing their tails in

William Lee

George Washington

contentment. Swallows had made nests in the top beams and seemed at home as they flew the span of the barn.

The smells and sights of this barn always made him think of his childhood. He worked hard at his mother's plantation, even as a boy. It was there that he was schooled in the various aspects of husbandry. Horses were his specialty. He learned how to train a horse. How to groom it, talk to it, gain its respect. He taught the young horses to accept a saddle and bridle. George Washington had a temper but learned that anger gets you nowhere with a horse. His natural leadership and athletic qualities, combined with his mastery of his emotions, had made him one of the best and most knowledgeable horsemen in Virginia.

Washington leaned against one of the stalls and reflected, "William Lee and I saw to the breaking of many a fine horse here. He was always good with the animals, seemed to understand them instinctively. He knew their language and appreciated their spirit. I recognized that talent in him shortly after I bought him. When he rode, he was one with the horse, fluid and loose. It was not very long before I brought him along to the fox hunts. He is a quick learner and he took to it right away. Good with the hounds too. He had a natural way of pulling them together and ushering them toward the scent of the fox.

"He was my match at the ride. He could run through woods, jump stonewalls, race through creeks. He made decisions quickly and did not need to be told what to do. Sometimes in early winter we did not wait for the hunt but rose before dawn and raced through stubble fields just to feel the horse under us and the sky above us. Once during one of those runs we spotted the black fox that had recently been seen in the area. As I began the chase, Billy warned me never to kill the black fox. He was so earnest about it that I called off the hounds. I don't think we ever saw that fox again. That was a long time ago." He sighed. "Now both of us are approaching the end of the trail."

The temperature had fallen and the snow had thickened while he was in the barn. Time in his barn had not dried his clothes. They still clung to his skin. Ignoring the discomfort, he headed now for Muddy Hole Farm. He wanted to speak with Davy Gray, his overseer. Davy looked after daily operations, made sure that workers were doing their job thoroughly and quickly, provided rations to them and punishments for infractions.

Washington usually hired white overseers from the neighborhood but complained that they drank too much, slept too late, and entertained their friends too often. Not Davy Gray. Davy had come to Mount Vernon as one of Martha Washington's slaves when he was sixteen. He was a field worker, noticed by the General and eventually promoted to overseer. In 1793 Washington wrote, "Davy at Muddy Hole carries on his business as well as the white overseer and with more quietness than any of them. With proper directions he will do very well."

And he did do well. His position came with benefits: He wore leather breeches instead of the field worker's coarse linen. Occasionally he received cash gifts and extra quantities of food.

Like other farm slaves, Davy lived in a one-room cabin, but his had a brick chimney while the others had wooden ones that were subject to catching fire. The typical cabin also had leaky roofs and dirt floors. Children slept on the floor and adults on pallets attached to the wall. Davy had his own garden and raised turkeys and chickens, some of which he sold to Lucy in the Mansion's kitchen. What he did not have was freedom.

Davy saw the General approaching his cabin. He quickly opened the door and told one of his sons to take the horse to the barn.

"Welcome, Master," he said. "Come in and get warm." Davy's wife, Molly, came forward, curtseyed, and with her head lowered said, "Good morning, Master."

"Thank you, Davy," said Washington. "The warmth of your cabin is most welcome. And Molly, I see that you have been spinning. That is a very good winter occupation. We need to have three hundred yards for the plantation and several more to send abroad.

"And now, Davy, tell me about Muddy Hole Farm."

"Well, Master," replied Davy, "things here seem to be running smoothly. We have been threshing wheat and husking corn."

"And the cornstalks?"

"Yes, Master, they are nearly all cut down. I was just getting ready to meet the hands in the field so the job could get finished."

"Have you finished filling the pens with leaves?"

"Yes, sir, I put several hands on that and they will be done tomorrow. Then we will start making a pen to winter the colts. I have five hands that will go with me to kill and clean the hogs. If the hunt goes well, they will be available for Christmas at the house. Next week I plan to see that the wood is cut for Christmas and begin to make the posts and rails for fencing."

"A very fine schedule," said the General. "It will work well. Tell me, Davy, how many children are at Muddy Hole?"

"There are nineteen children here," said Davy softly. All the slaves knew they could be sold away from their families at any time, adults and children, at the whim of their owner, like farm

William Lee   15

animals or bales of cotton. It was their worst fear, even though it was widely known that here at Mount Vernon, the master was reluctant to separate families and had instructed his farm managers to keep families together when selling slaves.

"That is good to hear," said the General, smiling. As the words left his mouth his brain recalled the advertisement he had seen many years ago during a trip to Williamsburg. It appeared in the Virginia Gazette in 1769. He had never forgotten it.

THIRTY choice VIRGINIA born SLAVES
Consisting chiefly of boys and girls
From 14 or 15 down to the ages
Of two or three years
Credit will be given

Washington, thirty-seven at the time, had been buying and selling human beings for many years. This touched his soul. It meant that a slave trader had purposely looked for children to sell, tearing them away from their parents and all they knew. In most cases they would never see them again. He remembered William Lee had accompanied him on that trip and because Washington had permitted him to learn to read, he knew what the ad said. Washington remembered watching tears roll down his valet's cheeks.

"Was that when it began?" he wondered. "When I began to accept the humanity of slaves? Was that it?"

Turning to Davy, he said, "You know families stay together at Mount Vernon?"

"Yes, Master," said Davy quietly.

"I must be on my way," said the General. "Keep up the good

work, Davy."

"Yes, Master," replied Davy, bowing slightly.

George Washington

Chapter Two
WILLIAM LEE

Thursday
December 12, 1799
6 a.m.

The penetrating cold and fog seeped into the slave barracks next to the greenhouse close by the Mansion. A man inside rolled over in the lower bunk and pulled up a blanket. From his position, he could see the last embers in the hearth. Today he would have to find someone to bring more wood. He knew his fellow Mansion slaves well and one of them would do that for him.

As he lay waiting to find the energy to rise, random thoughts spilled into consciousness. He remembered the day the General came to the Lee plantation, the day of the auction, the day that brought plantation owners and neighbors together. It was a day to hear the news of the area and of England. The smell of food permeated the grounds: chicken stew, sausage with apples, bacon and fried tomatoes, biscuits, apple pie, offered to customers to show the seller's hospitality. The smell was all that was offered to

William Lee   19

the people who were for sale. He remembered standing on the auction block in the freshness of a Virginia October morning. He could hear the geese honking as they returned to Chesapeake Bay for the winter and he could hear the auction gavel come down as another slave was sold. The enticing aromas of food made his mouth water and reminded him that he had not eaten this day. People came forward and felt his muscles, told him to open his mouth so they could check for disease, asked for him to be walked around so they could make sure he was not crippled. He remembered trying to control the anger of a sixteen-year-old. Displaying anger would only lead to the whipping post. He had often been a witness to that. He remembered the stifled cries of his mother as she was bought and taken away. He remembered her agonized look as she was led past him and placed in a cart, hands tied together, taken to who knows where. He had not seen her since. He wondered for the five hundredth time whether she was still alive.

The auction was taking place because the Widow Lee had debts to pay. The easiest way to address that was to sell her slaves. William and his brother, Frank, were part of the property being sold.

"That was the first time I saw the General," William remembered. "I thought what a mighty man he was, so tall and athletic and he sat on his horse with ease. He looked me over real well and asked me a few questions. I answered without hesitating. I remember he bid 61 pounds for me and 50 pounds for Frank. Imagine—111 pounds was the value of two mulatto boys. Boys whose father was either the master, or the master's son, or the overseer, or a casual acquaintance who was staying at the plantation. My mother never said, probably because she didn't know. She was forced to be available to satisfy the physical desires of any man who came to the cabin. I remember her look of fear when in the middle of the night we would hear the thump of heavy boots and the creak of the door as a strange man entered and called out for my mother. As soon as we heard those boots, Mama would cover us with a blanket. 'Hide now,' she would say. 'The man is coming and he does not like seeing the children. Hide under the blanket real good now. Be very quiet.' We would do as she said, but we could still hear the noises. Noises of bodies moving and a man grunting. And when he left and we could come out of hiding, we could see the silent tears rolling down Mama's cheeks. Sometimes, in the summer when it was warm, a man would take her outside for a while, but the tears still rolled. I have been told that in the old days a mulatto child inherited the status of his father. That means that I would be free and able to have my own life. But when the folks realized that if they continued that practice, slavery would die, the men quickly changed the law and I inherited the status of my mother, slave.

"That day, they tied our hands behind our backs and ordered us to get in the cart that would take us to Mount Vernon. They did not give us a chance to say good-bye to anyone. They did not want to allow emotions to be stirred up. This was a business deal. Frank and I had no idea what lay ahead, what our jobs would be, who the overseer would be, where we would be housed. We were now General Washington's property and he could do with us as he wished. We were both apprehensive, but we tried not to show it. A sobbing slave never got his way.

"I suppose that was about thirty years ago. So much has

happened since. Things a young slave boy would never have dreamed of. And now here I am: an old man with two broken knees, barely able to walk, and still a slave.

"The General bought two more boys that day, Adam and Jack. They were young; he only paid 19 pounds each for them. He probably figured they were a good investment. In a few more years they would be full grown and ready for the fields. He could sell them for much more than he paid. They put us all in the cart and headed toward Mount Vernon. The boys were particularly upset, for they were being taken from their mothers and all they had ever known. Frank and I knew enough to whisper to them not to show their sadness and to be brave. But as the cart rolled and pitched down the rutted road, I wondered what the future held for all of us.

"As we passed the Washington properties we could see many slaves working in the fields, bringing in the fall harvest. They were watched by a 'driver' who made sure they were working hard and long. He carried a short whip on his belt that he used freely if he thought a slave was not doing his job well enough or fast enough. I noticed that day there were many women working in the fields; that was not the case at the Lee plantation. I was to later learn that most of the Washington slaves were considered skilled workers, trained as coopers, blacksmiths, cooks, or valets. Because our mother had worked in the Lees' house, we knew the difference between field work and work in the big house. We knew what was expected and what we could expect. We knew how to interpret the white folks, not only what they said but what they meant. We knew that whatever we witnessed we had to keep to ourselves. And we knew that if we worked in the house, we had opportunities for better food and clothing. Mama had trained us how to be a slave, how to anticipate our owners' desires and needs, how to stay alive, and also how to hope, and somewhere deep inside how to find your soul and celebrate life. 'The owners can take your body but not your soul,' she used to say. She told us 'If you don't celebrate life it will die inside you.' We came well prepared. Adam and Jack had much to learn.

"When we arrived at Mount Vernon, we were put in the slave quarters that first night, still anxious. The following morning, we were taken into the kitchen and introduced to the cook and her helpers. After a small breakfast the General came in and said he was in need of a body servant—someone who would help him dress, carry messages, provide for all his personal needs. I knew exactly what this meant and was relieved that this is what lay in store for me. Frank, he said, would be working in the kitchen and the dining room. This was good news, for it meant we would not be separated. I would dress in the red and white livery that had been custom made to match the Washington coat of arms. I would also have shoes with buckles. For a young slave like me, this was a great opportunity, and I was determined to make the most of it.

"That very day, he asked me if I knew how to ride a horse. I answered that I had been around horses since I was a child and that the Lees at times had me be their jockey at races. I did not tell him that horses were the only thing that let me know what freedom was. It was when I celebrated life. Riding a horse at a gallop over fields and across streams let me be in control. I could not control my life but I could control a horse.

"That day and in the following weeks, I rode with him and was tested by him. I could see he was pleased I understood horses as well as he did. Soon he was introducing me to his beloved hunting

William Lee

hounds. Showing me how to handle them at the fox hunt, how to help them find the scent of the fox, how to see when they were aching to be let loose to follow the scent and how to get them to respond to the sound of the horn. The hound and the horse were two creatures he cherished. He took part in three hunts a week in those days. Sometimes he would be joined by a few of his friends or sometimes it was just the General and me.

"One of those times when it was just the two of us, we raced across the fields at a heady clip and I won the race. He looked at me and laughed. 'You know that if I bought you, I can sell you.' He thought it was funny, but to a slave it was not. I did not have the freedom to reply, so I kept silent.

"After the hunt the traditional breakfast would be ready for the guests. And what a breakfast it was! It started with bourbon and was followed by eggs, sausage, sweetbreads, oysters, chicken, stew, bacon and fried tomatoes, herring, ham, and biscuits. I was told I could find breakfast in the kitchen. A slave never ate with the white folks. This was a better breakfast than the gruel provided to those who worked on the other properties belonging to the General.

"As I learned more and more, he put me charge of the hounds and I became the kennel-huntsman, caring for the hounds and directing them at the hunt. He used to say to me that a good foxhound is like a good soldier. He stays in perfect formation until he is told to attack. He is not distracted by other prey and does not run off to chase them. He follows the commands of his general. The hounds are disciplined, loyal, and eager to please. I did not know then that in the future we would both see the hounds replaced with young men on the battlefield.

William Lee   25

"Sometimes we would see the black fox. We would chase him right away. Usually he would outrun us, but there was one time when we had him cornered and the General was ready to send the hounds in for the kill. 'Excuse me, Master,' I said. 'You should never kill a black fox. He is the smartest of all foxes. Bad luck to kill the black fox.' The General looked at me with interest and then called the hounds off."

William Lee rolled over in his bunk and swung his feet to the floor. This was the hardest part of getting up. Over the years his knees had deteriorated badly following separate injuries, making it very difficult for him to walk. "It is these bad knees that kept me from serving the General when he was president," William recalled. "I did try to go with him, but it was very clear I could not do the service I had always done for him. So I was sent back here to Mount Vernon to fix shoes."

He pulled himself up and grabbed the crutches that were at the end of the bed. He made his way to an area where he could relieve himself and wash. Others around him were also rising, all of them slaves, all of them working at the Mansion or its dependencies. These were the privileged slaves, spared the endless backbreaking labor in the fields, the sparse cabins and minimal rations. Most could not read or write, education was not encouraged. This would have identified them as more than mere slaves and given proof that they were indeed humans. As William Lee left the greenhouse slave quarters, the cold dampness of the day penetrated his bones. He was heading for the kitchen. To prevent the spread of fire, it was housed in a building that was separate from the Mansion, connected by a covered walkway. His brother Frank, who came with him all those years ago, was married to Lucy the cook. They had three children. Lucy and the children were under the control of Mrs. Washington and Frank was owned by the General. Frank was still the butler in the house, always ready to be of service at any hour of the day or night and always discerning about keeping silent or speaking quietly to the master. Lucy would be preparing breakfast for the household. Frank would be setting the table. William Lee knew that his special standing would allow Lucy to give him breakfast as well. The large kitchen fireplace warmed him and gave him comfort. As Lucy handed William a plate of eggs, bacon, and toast, Frank came into the kitchen and greeted his brother with a strong handshake.

"You are the one who can answer the question," he said. "Last night a few of us were discussing the war and wondering if the General ever permitted black folk in the army. Do you know?"

"I do know," he answered. "I heard part of the discussion several times. Right at the beginning when the General first became head of the Continental Army, he made it clear that no Negroes, slave or free, were to be soldiers in his army. Slaves in the army might be a threat to slaveholders in many of the colonies. What was of more importance was that he wanted his army to be professional, dignified and educated. Slaves had none of these qualities. Somehow that did not apply to me. I was his valet and continued in that position throughout the war. I still wore the red and white livery of the Washington family, not the buff and blue of the army. I was by his side at all times. I think, as his valet, I knew more than many who held important positions. We all know when to be quiet, don't we?" he said, winking at all the slaves around him.

"Finally, I think it must have been around November of 1775, the General issued an order that no Negroes, boys too young to

28 *George Washington*

bear arms, or old men were to be enlisted. But then that man, Lord Dunmore, told slaves that if they joined the British army they would be given their freedom. That was quite an offer, and many of our brothers took it."

"And some of them are free today," said Frank quietly.

"And some are not," said Lucy. "Do you remember when that British ship was right out there in the river and offered freedom to any slave who would come to their side?"

"I do remember that," said Frank. "It was a hard choice. Seventeen of the master's slaves took the offer and boarded the boat."

"But when the war ended, seven of them were sent right back here to Mount Vernon. Don't know what happened to the other seven. Maybe they made it to Canada. But the seven that were sent back still work at hard labor in the fields," said Lucy.

"Well, the end of the story," said William Lee, "is that about month after the General said no Negroes in the army, he changed his mind and said free blacks, not slaves, could join. That's when it became official. I watched them fight bravely. I really did. I think the count was about five thousand free blacks were enlisted."

Lucy looked at Frank. The mistress would come to the kitchen soon to order the meals for the day. They'd better look busy.

William understood what that look meant and recovered his crutches. "I should be getting to work too," he said. "Thanks for the hearty breakfast," he said as he gave his sister-in-law a brief hug.

William Lee

Chapter Three
TABLE TALK

Thursday
December 12, 1799
1 p.m.

As the General closed Davy's cabin door, he checked his pocket watch and saw that it was two o'clock. The main meal at Mount Vernon was always served at three. That meant he must head back.

The General was extremely punctual and today would be no exception. The temperature was dropping and it had begun to hail. By the time he reached the Mansion, his clothes were saturated with snow and rain and his hair matted under his hat. There might be guests for dinner, he thought. It seemed there were always guests for dinner. Since he retired, slightly over two years before, Mount Vernon had hosted some six hundred visitors. But today there were no carriages or horses in front of the house.

"The weather must have kept people away," he thought. "It will be a welcome quiet dinner."

Frank had set the mahogany table in the green dining room and

George Washington

provided enough candles to brighten the cold, gray day. A fire was roaring in the fireplace.

Spits of hail and snow accompanied the General as he opened the front door. Christopher quickly took his master's wet coat and pulled his boots off, offering him a dry pair of shoes. He would not keep the family waiting by taking time to change his clothes. Christopher then brought him a glass of whiskey from the plantation's distillery mixed with hot water to take the chill off.

Soon the servants began to quietly bring in a parade of dishes: a small roasted pig, some fish, potatoes, carrots, puddings and tarts. Joining the General and his wife at the table was his secretary and longtime friend, Tobias Lear.

Lear had been hired at the age of twenty-three by the Washingtons as a tutor to Martha's grandchildren and as a personal secretary to the General. He was quickly embraced by the family and became Washington's right-hand man and confidant. Ever loyal, he often spoke of Washington's honesty, uprightness, and candor He had great admiration for Martha Washington as well and regarded her almost as a second mother. Lear took care of financial matters, wrote letters that the General dictated, sent invitations for dinner, and organized the numberless papers. He had been married twice and widowed twice, his wives taken by the communicable diseases prevalent at the time, yellow fever and tuberculosis. He had one son by his first marriage, Benjamin Lincoln Lear, whose godfather was George Washington. Currently, at the age of thirty-seven, Tobias was unmarried.

Frank held the chair for Mrs. Washington while Tobias and the General took their places. "We shall pray," said the General.

By his hands are we all fed.
Thank you for our daily bread.

After the Amens, the General asked, "And how is the new mother?" Martha's granddaughter Nelly and her baby girl were being cared for by Caroline in a bedroom upstairs. Nelly's husband, Lawrence Lewis, was away on business.

"She is doing just fine," answered Martha. "Getting more strength every day. It is a joy to have her here, and the baby is very healthy and strong. Did you hear her crying last night?"

"I did not," said the General, "but I am not sure that men are alert to the needs of infants.

"I went out to the sixteen-sided barn today," he said, pushing back his wet hair. "I must say, even if I did design it, it is a fine barn. Brought back a host of memories, especially memories about William Lee. Did I ever tell you the story about the Massachusetts boys and the Virginia boys?"

"I don't think you have," said Tobias as he took a sip of wine. "People have mentioned it to me, but I would like to hear about it straight from you."

Outside it was cloudy and cold. Hail clattered against the windows, and as the wind picked up, branches of nearby trees rubbed against the house. The General stretched his long legs under the table and leaned back in his chair. "Well, let me see. It was right after I was named commander-in-chief of the Continental Army in 1775. I left Philadelphia, went to New York and on to Boston. Shortly after I arrived, I visited the army camps. I was not prepared for what I found. The men were unruly, undisciplined, and did not like taking orders. Their latrines were disgusting and they themselves were filthy. Their quarters were

William Lee   33

made of boards, or sailcloth, or stone and turf, or even of birch and brush. It would be a big task to develop discipline and order."

" 'Tis good I wasn't there yet," said Martha as she signaled Frank to pass the rolls around.

"Around the end of July, troops from Virginia arrived, led by Captain Daniel Morgan," the General continued. "They had walked six hundred miles to join the Continental Army. They wore ruffled linen shirts and leather leggings and carried long rifles. Well, the boys from Massachusetts dressed in fishermen's jackets and trousers did not take kindly to these fancy boys and taunted them for several months, until one snowy winter day a real fight broke out between the two groups. Snowballs at first, but then it became fisticuffs, eye gouging, and biting. There were over a thousand men in the fight. When I was informed about it at headquarters, I told William Lee to accompany me, and the two of us made our way to the scene. We rode right into the thick of it and I jumped from my horse, grabbed two of them by the neck, held them at arm's length, shook them and talked to them. At the same time, William Lee moved our horses right into the melee. His skill with horses was instinctive; he knew just what to do, making the participants move back and apart. Immediately all the rest of the combatants began to scatter. It would not happen again soon."

Frank, standing against the wall watching to see what the diners might need, smiled as the name of his brother came up at the table.

"You know, William was right there with me throughout the war. He carried my spyglass, helped me dress, combed my hair, slept on a pallet outside my tent, delivered important documents, rode next to me in battle. And he knew what he was doing. Yes, William saw me at my best and at my worst. Yes, indeed."

"Did you ever admit Negroes into the army?" asked Tobias.

"At first I did not, but when Lord Dunmore was offering freedom to slaves who came to the British side and when I saw how many free Negroes were fighting from Massachusetts, Rhode Island, and other places, I changed my mind and accepted free Negroes into all the units. It was a good decision."

"What about the Negroes who were slaves and not free?" asked Tobias.

Coughing, the General answered, "That was a point of contention for many. The Southern colonies were afraid to arm their slaves for fear of rebellion, and yet sometimes they would send a slave to the army instead of coming themselves. The slave soldiers were very good and able to follow the commands, you know. They just needed training."

"And was William with you at the Delaware?"

"Yes, indeed." The General smiled. "What a night that was. If you think I am wet now, you should have seen us then. While you were snug at home Christmas night, Mr. Lear, my men marched with me to the Delaware River. Some of them did not have shoes, their feet were bleeding, they were cold and hungry, but still they marched and waited for commands. William was right there fetching guns, looking for opportunities to help make our march successful, doing whatever I told him to do, quickly and without question. He even helped find boats for the crossing.

"The New Englanders saved the whole plan. They came with cargo boats, large enough to carry horses and men and equipment. And they were skilled at night crossings. A howling nor'easter was blowing and the river was freezing up. We had to get cannon, men, and horses into the boats to cross the three hundred yards of water.

William's skill with horses kept them from panicking and they moved quite willingly onto those cargo boats.

"We tried to move in complete silence, but I will not forget the sound of the ice floes as they cracked against each other in that dark river."

"And all the while, I was enjoying the holiday," said Tobias as Frank filled his wineglass.

"Well, you were just a boy," said Martha. "Your mother was probably happy you were with her. I was here at Mount Vernon that night, finally relaxing after the Christmas festivities. Everyone here missed the presence of the General. Of course, we had no way of knowing what was going on. The whole plan was secret, but we all knew he would be with us if it was possible. I did join him at Morristown in March."

Clearing his throat and reaching for the bottle of Madeira, the General continued, "When we finally made it to the other side of the Delaware, with the wind and the snow roaring around us, we still had to march another ten miles. Those tired, hungry, freezing men marched on with determination and belief in what they were fighting for. Looking back, it is amazing that they could keep going."

"You were looking for the Hessians, those hirelings of the British, is that right?" Tobias asked.

"Yes, we were, and when we did find them, they were caught completely off guard, never believing we would cross the river in that kind of weather. After a brief skirmish,—less than an hour—they surrendered. And did we help ourselves to Christmas presents! We took muskets, bayonets, cannon, horses, and swords, along with a great deal of rum and nine hundred prisoners. I can

William Lee

truly say that every Christmas since, I've thought of that night with enormous appreciation for what my men did."

"Did you ever have any reservations about the attack?" asked Tobias.

"I did indeed but was able to ignore them. And I had a confident trust that we would not be ignored by heaven."

"But sir," said Tobias, "what if it hadn't worked?"

"It probably would have been the end of the rebellion and I would have been hunted down, captured, returned to England as a traitor, then drawn and quartered and my head put on a pike on London Bridge. All those who signed the Declaration of Independence would have been hanged and all their property confiscated, including their slaves."

"But did you have a plan to escape capture?"

"Well, I did, but I am not sure how practical it was. I planned to run and hide in the Ohio Country and beyond. The British lack the woodsman skills that area demands and I thought I could outfox them. Martha would have had to go with me; otherwise they would have taken her hostage. They would have burned our beloved Mount Vernon to the ground. William Lee always said he would be by my side if it came to that. I am not sure my plan would have worked, though. Perhaps Lafayette could have taken us to France and given us refuge there.

"May I have more tea, Frank? I am getting chilled."

"Yes, sir; right away, sir."

"Now my dear old man, you sound like you are coming down with something. I have a tonic Dr. Craik gave us. Why don't you put a bit in your tea?" asked Martha.

"I will be fine," said the General. "Don't you fret."

Suddenly the sound of music drifted in from the New Room across the hall. The General had added this room to the Mansion in order to entertain the many people who came to visit. It was large enough to serve numerous people at the long table and could accommodate music and dancing as well. Full of light from several two-story Palladian windows, it was an inviting space. However, on this snowy afternoon only soft light entered.

Leaving the table to find the source of the music, the three diners were delighted to see Nelly at the harpsichord. Caroline held the baby and crooned as the melody filled the room.

"Oh, Frank, we need a fire here," said Martha. "We can't let the child get cold."

"Yes, ma'am! I will do that right now."

"I am so much better," said Nelly. "I was starting to feel caged in. I thought a little music would help."

"And you look better," said the General. "What a treat to have you play. Martha, would you do me the honor of dancing with me?"

"Now George, aren't we getting a bit old for that?"

"Indeed not," he answered. "You know how I love to dance."

"Yes, of course I do. Your ability on the dance floor was one of the things that first attracted me to you, old man."

"Well, then, shall we?" The General bowed and took his wife's hand. As the snow fell against the frosted windows and the fire crackled in the fireplace, the devoted couple danced and laughed.

"George," exclaimed Martha, "your clothes are still wet and I am getting wet too. And your voice is raspy."

Nelly, Tobias, Frank, and Caroline all smiled. It was a special moment to watch these two who had endured so much: the loss of Martha's children, the loss of all their siblings, months of separation, the unending fear of capture and death . . . And still they could still laugh and dance.

"Go on now," said Martha. "Change your clothes and get to bed."

"Yes, yes," he replied, "but first I want to do a bit of work at my desk. I will take my tea there, Frank."

Crossing the hall, he saw Sweetlips curled by the fire. "Shh," he said. "The mistress is still about."

As was his habit, he entered the weather in his diary.

Morning snowing and ab't 3 Inches deep. Wind at No. Et & Mer at 30. Con'd snowing till 1 O'clock and ab't 4 it became perfectly clear. Wind in the same place but not hard. Mer 28 at night.

After writing a while longer, he finally made his way to bed.

William Lee 41

Chapter Four

OTHER OBSERVATIONS

Thursday
December 12, 1799

10 a.m.

William left the kitchen and hobbled through the rain and slush to his small workshop behind the greenhouse. Here he mended and made shoes, an essential task for a plantation with over three hundred slaves. It was important to protect the feet of those who worked long hours, whether in the fields or in the Mansion. When William's knees gave out, the General set up this workshop for him and occasionally stopped in to check on his friend and to have a chat about old times.

Now William stoked the fire and found the right piece of leather to mend the split shoe in front of him. He settled into his chair and set to work.

As he cut the leather he could hear the sounds of the plantation and the morning routine starting up. The plantation manager

George Washington

would be meeting with the overseers, giving them orders for the day and checking on the condition of each of the General's five farms. William could hear their footsteps as they trudged through the slush toward the manager's office. He could also hear several of the young slave children laughing and throwing snowballs until admonished by their parents to come and help with work they had been assigned. A stray snowball missed its mark and hit the back door of the Mansion with a splat.

With that, the door opened and Christopher Sheels could be heard scolding the children. "Go on now," he said. "Get to your chores."

He entered the greenhouse quarters shaking his hat, saying, "Sometimes those kids sure do make trouble. Good to see you, William. Thought I could stop by for a bit. The General is out by himself checking on everything and everybody. Doesn't need me for a while." A young man of about twenty-four, he was tall and broad-shouldered and carried himself with poise and grace. He had a wide smile that immediately made you comfortable.

"Always good to see you," said William. "Sit down by the fire. Those kids and their snowballs made me think of Boston."

"And when was that?" asked Christopher. He had heard the old man's stories many times before, but he did not mind hearing them again. He found a chair by the fire and settled in.

"Seems just like yesterday," said William, "but it must be over twenty years ago." William laughed to himself. "That was some day," he mused. "Yes, indeed, some day. The General came out of headquarters and said, 'Come on, William, we are going to a snowball fight. I need my best uniform and my sword. It is important to look like a commander.'

William Lee   43

"Not sure why he needed a sword for a snowball fight, but I prepared his clothes, combed his hair, tied it at the back, and brought his always polished boots. Then I brought the horses around and we both mounted and headed to an open field near Harvard. As usual, I was carrying his spyglass always ready for him. 'Spyglass,' he called to me. I handed it to him, and as we approached the area he used it to see what was going on. And yes, indeed, our own boys were throwing snowballs at each other. Then it got worse, and they began to fight each other with fists and feet. The General, with his horse, went right into it. He was steady, large, and manly, and you thought twice before you disobeyed his command. I moved in with my horse and pushed the pack of scoundrels back and split it up. As soon as they saw the General, those boys ran off and the fight stopped. That was all it took, a big serious general, dressed to show he was in command. That was some day!"

William stood once again and walked to the fireplace to add another log. "Would have been most welcome to have a fire like this the night the General led us across the Delaware River. It was mighty cold. That wind was not so bad at first, but it grew and grew, causing problems for all of us. We marched in darkness that Christmas night. I was lucky. The general had given me good shoes and a greatcoat, but many had no shoes or warm clothing. But let me tell you, they would follow the General. He was always right with them in the fight, right out in front, and I was expected to be there with him. The men could look forward and see their General on his big white horse at the very front and they followed. But I tell you, getting those horses on the boats was not easy. They were cold too, and the sound of the wind and the splashing of the

William Lee

45

water spooked them. I had to use all my tricks to get them into the boat, and once I did, they began to lose their footing on decks that were freezing over. That spooked them even more. Besides that, the General wanted us to be very quiet so we could surprise those Hessians. Good thing it was snowing hard enough that it was almost impossible to spot us. Whew! Just thinking about it makes me cold again," he said, as he began to fit the leather to the shoe mold.

"Christopher, let me tell you something else about that night. I was right by the General and as he was directing the movement of some big guns. We were on a very slippery slope when his horse's hind legs buckled and he began to skid down the slope. I saw him twist the horse's mane, pull his head back, and shift his own weight so that the animal could regain his footing. It all happened so quickly. I tell you, to this day that man is a fine horseman."

"And did you surprise the enemy?" Christopher asked, even though he knew the answer.

"Yes, we surely did. They had no idea we were coming. The battle lasted only about an hour." He laughed as he recalled that wonderful day. "And I tell you, we came away with piles of ammunition, swords, cannon, and, best of all, rum, lots of it. First the General ordered the men not to drink it, but later he changed his mind and told them to have a few and toast the victory."

"You know, I have always wanted to ask you, William," said Christopher. "How was it to be a slave and fight with free men? Did you ever want to run? Go to the redcoats?"

"That is some question," William said quietly. "I think when I was fighting by the General's side, I felt free. But how does any slave know how that really feels? The fight itself put me in a position to make decisions, a position I did not normally have. If I was not his valet, I would never have had the experiences that I had. There were many opportunities for me to run, and I knew many secrets that the British would have paid a lot of money for. Yet I could not do that to the General. He taught me a lot, and I think I taught him as well. We grew to respect one another. Besides, if I'd switched sides I would have been uncomfortable. I had seen too much. I did not trust them."

"You must have thought about it?"

"Oh, I did, often. But I couldn't go through with it. One time in particular, we were camped on a hill near White Plains, New York. October, I think it was. Yes, it was October because I can still remember the colors of leaves in that part of the country. Although the leaves were pretty, the General and his army were not. We had had a long series of defeats and the men were hungry and extremely tired. They did not have tents or blankets, many of them made a bed out of piles of those beautiful leaves."

"Now Christopher, you know about the people that follow the army. They come along when it moves. There are quite few of them, some times as many as two thousand. They do things like wash the soldiers clothes or some of them are actually the families of the soldiers. We needed them but they often did not follow orders. That frustrated the General quite a bit. Sometimes if I needed something for the General like buttons or a razor I could find them among the camp followers who sold such things. So one evening I went looking for something. Can't remember just what it was but I went where the camp followers were. I was stopped by a man who motioned for me to follow. He was dressed like a peddler, quite small and appeared to be slightly built. He led me to a secluded spot behind some army wagons and then opened a sachel full of small items to sell.

As I looked at his wares he asked me if I was the General's valet."

"Yes," I replied. "I am looking for some buttons."

As I looked through his supply he said in low tones.

"Have you ever thought about getting out of here?"

"A slave aren't you? I mean the General owns you?"

"Yes," I answered in a whisper.

"I could get you out of here," he said. "And your freedom would come with money."

"What kind of money?"

"British money, more than you will ever need. You do take care of the General, right? You comb his hair, empty his chamber pots, fix his clothes, shine his shoes. Does anyone do that for you? No, you are just a slave."

"I could not think of an answer and stayed silent."

"If you came over to the right side, the British side, you might have enough money to buy your own slave. Make your own choices, any children you might have in the future would be free.

I dare say you must know lots of things like I bet you even know the battle plans and where the army will go next. The Brits would pay handsomely for that information."

"Did you want to accept the offer?" asked Christopher.

"I can't say I didn't think about it. Freedom and money, something I had always dreamed of. And yet I knew it could not be that easy. And I knew that the Brits did not always keep their word. I also knew that if I was caught I would be hung and there would be no mercy."

"So I just said I wasn't interested and all I wanted to do was buy a few buttons. The peddler agreed but told me if I changed my mind he would be at the same spot the next night. And as he walked away I saw a woman's skirt hanging out at the bottom of his coat."

"Do you think the peddler was really a woman?" asked Christopher.

"I am not sure but many years later I heard that a lady spy had hung around with the camp followers disguised as a peddler. She was able to get information for the Brits like how many cannons we had and what our brigades were doing. I would not be surprised if it was the same person who approached me that night."

"Did you ever regret not taking the offer? asked Christopher.

"Not really. I did not want to be at the end of a noose and I did not trust the Brits. I would rather be on General Washington's side."

As the fire crackled and the snow fell quietly outside, Christopher said softly, "I wonder what it is like to be really free."

"You are still a young man, Christopher. Maybe someday you will be free."

"Free to come and go when I wish? Choose my work? Free of punishment? Free to have life and liberty?" Christopher's voice was rising with frustration. "Free from asking permission even to marry? I long for dignity and respect. I can't believe it will ever happen. The white folks need us to carry on. Freeing us would end all they have. Who would let us go? Who?"

"I have heard of it happening, but not often. For some masters, their slaves are worth more than their lands. And then what would we do? Where would we work? Where would we live?"

"I would go north and find work, blend in with the community.

I could do it."

"I hear you made an attempt, Christopher."

"William, you know my wife lives on a plantation nearby. She sent me a letter with a plan to escape and I dropped it. Before I could go back and get it, the General found it. I was so afraid, for me, for my wife, for my life."

"Christopher, how old were you when you replaced me as the General's valet?"

"Fourteen."

"Fourteen? You were a kid. And didn't you see a lot with the General? New York, Philadelphia? Didn't he give you special treatment, clothes, shoes, good food? And didn't he find the best help for you when you were bitten by that rabid hound? Didn't he give permission for you to marry?"

"Yes, he gave me a good deal. Everything but freedom!" said the young man, his face filled with anger and resentment.

"He can't, because you belong to the Missus and the Custis estate. He can't free you. And he has not freed me either. I have been with him since before you were born. I have been by his side, always by his side. Always. Until these old knees gave out. But I was even by his side when that happened. It was on one of his surveying trips when I slid down a hill and hurt my knee.

"Did the General ever speak to you about the note?" William asked.

"Yes, one morning last summer he called me into his library. He had been working all morning on a pile of papers. And I was so frightened for me and my wife and my brothers and sisters. It was the kind of fear that keeps you from speaking or moving.

"He looked at me with disgust and said, 'Christopher, I am very

George Washington

disturbed to find this note. I will have to show it to your wife's master. And as for you, you have disappointed me a great deal, but this is one time I will let it pass. Go now,' he said, 'and don't ever try that again.'

"Did you not ever hear about Tom?" William asked. "Ran away twice. First time, the General forgave him. Second time, he paid a captain to take him to the Caribbean, where they have sugarcane fields, and sell him. I am telling you, Christopher, you do not want that. You go there and you live about four more years and then you die from the work. You have to watch yourself. You have already given him reason to be suspicious of you.

"And remember, you have it better than most of the slaves here. You don't have to sleep in a cabin with a dirt floor and a chimney that barely works. You get fine clothes while most of the folk only get two sets a year. Your food is way better than the field hands'. Get smart, young man. Be careful.

"You know," William continued, "my mama always used to say, They can take your body but they can't take your soul. That soul is yours and God gave it to you. I have always remembered that and it helps. It helps."

Christopher was standing by the fire with his back to William. William put down the shoe he was working on, rose, and placed his hand on the young man's shoulder. Christopher turned, embarrassed by the tears that ran down his young face. In silence he put his coat back on and said, "I just can't talk any more right now, William. Besides, it will soon be time for the master to return."

He wiped his face, went back out into the snow, and headed toward the Mansion.

William Lee 51

Chapter Five
A STAR-FILLED NIGHT

Friday
December 13, 1799
5 a.m.

The General woke as usual at five o'clock the next morning and saw three inches of snow covering the lawn that swept down to the river. Snow covered the stables, the garden, the slave quarters, the outbuildings. It made pyramids on the fence posts and hung heavily on the trees that lined the Mansion drive. It muffled the sound of the slaves as they made their way to their work under gray clouds. It was still snowing.

He was not as refreshed as he normally was after a good night's sleep. Coughing and a sore throat had kept him awake amid intermittent dreams of past battles. Dreams full of billowing clouds of smoke and bright flashes of light. He could almost taste the black gunpowder that hung in the air. He heard the commands:

William Lee   53

"Prime and load! Shoulder! Make ready! Aim and fire!" And he heard the shrill screams: of the horses shot and collapsing in agony, of the men as they took a bullet or a bayonet. He heard the clashing of swords and the swearing of soldiers as they met their enemy.

Coughing still, he rose in the soft morning light and began his usual routine of washing, finding Sweetlips, going to his study, prayer and paperwork, followed by breakfast. He ate little, complaining of a sore throat and runny nose.

"I won't be riding out today," he said.

"I am happy to hear that," Martha replied. "You are in no condition to go out in this weather."

The General smiled and thought about all the different kinds of weather his body had endured: summers so hot some of his men died of sunstroke, torrential rain that muddied roads and soaked the body, icy winter storms. What was a cough and a sore throat to an old soldier?

Later, in the afternoon, he ignored his wife's concern and told Christopher he would dress to go outside. "I need to inspect the ha-ha wall that keeps the animals from wandering onto the lawn. It appears I will need my greatcoat."

Accompanied by Sweetlips, he exited through the back door, took a deep breath, and drank in the scene. The Potomac flowed silently at the foot of the lawn. Caked with ice floes, it still pulsated with the many forms of life that lay beneath its rolling waters. He could hear the rigging on the boats tied up at the wharf as it hit the masts. In the distance, the barking of several hounds penetrated the falling snow.

The river was not only beautiful, it facilitated a great deal of commerce. Its waters teemed with fish: herring, bass, sturgeon, and whitefish, available as rations to his slaves and also sold by the barrelful to the West Indies.

He stood now looking at the water, and for some reason, perhaps because of his dreams the night before, he thought of the Battle of Yorktown, the final battle of the Revolution, the battle that ended the war.

The British had retreated to the southern tip of Virginia on Chesapeake Bay. Under the command of Cornwallis, they occupied a small strip of land between the James and the York rivers. At the same time, the French had come to the aid of the Americans, providing much needed money, men, weapons, and ships.

The French general, Rochambeau, and Washington had devised a plan to attack the British where they were encamped at Yorktown, Virginia. The French admiral, de Grasse, sent word that he would be sailing from the West Indies with a fleet of twenty-eight ships of the line but would only be able to stay a month. This meant that while the French navy kept the British from escaping by sea, the French and American armies could attack where Cornwallis was camped. To do this, they came together and began the march south. They moved through New Jersey, Pennsylvania, Maryland, to the north point of Chesapeake Bay. There they were met by a flotilla of various boats that carried them down the bay to Williamsburg.

The two armies marched in stark contrast. The French were well trained, well fed, well dressed, and well armed. Washington's army consisted of men of every age, some as young as fifteen, white and black, sometimes poorly fed and certainly poorly

William Lee   55

uniformed. But they were determined and they were led by a man they admired. They understood why they were fighting.

As the snow continued to fall and Sweetlips chased a squirrel across the lawn, Washington remembered his arrival in Yorktown. William Lee handed him his spyglass, his face full of disgust. The General positioned it toward the York River. He could see over four hundred horses floating in the water in various stages of decay. The stench was intolerable. The British, having run out of food for the animals, solved the problem by herding them into the river, shooting them, and leaving them to rot. For a man who understood and valued horses, this was a cruel and unnecessary action. He turned away in anger. However, he knew this was one of the many signs that the British were in trouble. Without horses they could not get far.

Feeling a bit feverish but not really ill, the General stood in the soft falling snow and thought of the night of October 14, 1781. His army had swelled to 15,000, consisting of Americans, French, and the many militiamen from Virginia who had come to help. The British numbered about 6,000. For three weeks the allies had been consistently, methodically attacking the British fortifications. The patriots stood in awe as the French used their superior cannon and precise guns to take each entrenched British position. Then the allies devised a plan to attack at night. The General ordered his soldiers to "act the part of firm and brave soldiers. Attack silently; only use bayonets. We want the attack to be a surprise."

The First Rhode Island, mainly free black men, led the charge and took the British fortification. "They were so very cool and firm," the General remembered. Then at ten o'clock on the morning of October 17, a British drummer boy appeared on the top of a fortification, waving a white flag, followed by an officer, also waving a flag of surrender. The General smiled thinking of that day. The world's most powerful army surrendered to a ragtag crew whose belief in self-government had sustained them through five years of conflict.

As he moved across the snow-clad lawn, various ghostly images appeared before him in the mist: Alexander Hamilton, John Laurens, Lafayette, all dressed as officers, all smiling.

"Yes, we did it. Didn't we? We did it!" the General said. "And do you remember that night? A clear sky full of thousands and thousands of stars, with many meteors gleaming through the atmosphere. It was as if God Himself led the celebration."

And then, as he turned toward the house, he saw his stepson, Jack Custis, lingering on his deathbed. He had begged Washington to take him as a volunteer to Yorktown. Jack was inexperienced, vain, cocky, undisciplined. The General tried to find a way to dissuade him but eventually relented, even though Martha was very much against the plan. During the few weeks Jack was at Yorktown, he contracted camp fever. He suffered with high temperature, chills, headache, and rapid breathing. His condition was so serious, he was taken by cart to Martha's sister's plantation at Eltham, thirty miles away. When the battle had eased at Yorktown, the General took the opportunity to go Eltham to visit Jack. On his arrival he found that Martha was already there, as was Jack's young wife. As he entered the room where his stepson lay, he knew the young man did not have much time left. Within hours, the young man died in the presence of his wife, mother, and stepfather. Now all of Martha's children were gone. She was overcome with grief for all four of them, for the family they represented, for everything death destroyed.

Remembering that moment as he stood in the snow at Mount Vernon eighteen years later filled the General with great sadness. Jack's death had left a mark that could not be erased.

Coughing heavily, the General called to Sweetlips and together they went back to the house.

That evening, as was their custom, Martha, Tobias, and the General gathered for tea in the West Parlor. Frank brought some of the cold meats and desserts left from dinner, hot tea along with a bit of whiskey for the General's cough. Martha worked on her cross-stitch for the dining room chairs while her husband began to read the mail that had come that day. Despite his congestion, he was in a cheerful mood and read aloud from some of the newspapers that had arrived. As his voice grew weaker, he asked Tobias to do the reading. He was upset to learn that James Madison had nominated James Monroe for Virginia governor and had a few caustic remarks. Eventually Martha announced that she was going to bed and advised her husband to do the same.

"Come now, my old man. It is time for you to take that cold to bed," she said.

"I will be there soon," he replied.

Once she had left the room, Washington said to Tobias, "I saw some old friends on the lawn today."

"And who would that be, sir?"

"John Laurens, Lafayette, and Alexander Hamilton. I know it was just an old man's mirage, but they seemed so real. I miss those young men."

"Sometimes memories certainly do seem real," said Tobias.

"What a fine group of men. Did you know they all tried to

convince me to sell my slaves and tried to end slavery itself?"

"I think you understand my feelings about it," said Tobias as he stoked the fire. "I abhor the system and hope it will end in my lifetime."

"Laurens had a plan right from the beginning," the General replied. "He proposed to arm the slaves and give them freedom in exchange for their service in the Revolution. He proposed it three times to the South Carolina legislature. Failed all three times. He said 'We have sunk the Africans and their descendants below the standard of humanity.' "

"And I agree," said Tobias. "Hadn't his family been in the slave trade for many years?"

"Yes, they sold thousands of them. I think the young Laurens tried to convince his father to get out of the business, but he never did. Henry Laurens died just a few years ago. Never did free his slaves. John said, more than a few times, 'We can't fight for liberty until we have freed our slaves.' "

"John Laurens was a good soldier," the General continued, struggling to talk through his cough. "He led a battalion under Hamilton to storm the British position at Yorktown. Smart, too. I named him to the committee to draft formal terms for the British surrender. He spoke fluent French. He was perfect for that important job.

"He died in battle, young, only twenty-eight," the General went on, "killed in a skirmish under Nathanael Greene. He loved his country and what it stood for. If he had lived, I am convinced he would have done all that he could to end slavery.""I daresay Lafayette would have stood with John Laurens," said Tobias. "I often heard him call for the slaves to be freed."

"Lafayette—now, there is a story," said the General. "A young man who knew what he wanted and went after it. He was born into a French nobel family. Married into nobility as well, at sixteen. When he heard and read about the revolution here, he made his way to our shores."

"I am only five years younger than he," said Tobias. "I found him to be very sociable. Loved to flatter everyone. Gave everyone the French greeting, a kiss on each cheek."

"He did do that. Even the first time I met him. Made me uncomfortable. When he arrived at our camp, he asked to join the Continental Army. He was an outstanding horseman, trained at Versailles from a young age. I saw military talent in him, and within a year I made him a general. It was a feather in our cap to have a member of French nobility join the cause. I have often wondered what King George and Louis of France thought of this young man. It was not just an adventure to Lafayette. He believed in freedom and the inalienable rights of men," said Washington as he put more wood on the fire and wrapped himself in a shawl Martha had left behind. He was beginning to feel chilled and his cough was heavier.

"Lafayette had a plan to end slavery," said the General. "He wanted the two of us to buy a piece of property, free a few slaves at first, and then permit them to be tenants on the land, teach them how to farm. He even said that if it was successful, he would use the method in the West Indies.

"It was certainly an interesting proposal. I am principled against this kind of traffic in the human species. In fact, when I look back at my life, my greatest regret is that I participated in it. But I think the only way to abolish it is by legislative action."

"At this point that would be hard to come by," said Tobias.

"The state of New York did it just this past July. Its law says that all slave children born after July 4, 1799, will be free but will have to serve as indentured servants until they are young adults. The French were able to end all slavery, just five years ago. I am sure Lafayette must have had some influence. He is a good man. The son I never had. Named his own son after me."

"Did he not send you the Key to the Bastille that is in the case in the hall?"

"Yes, yes he did," said Washington. "It is symbolic of our history and relationship. I have the letter that accompanied it right here in a special place," he said as he rose from his chair and opened a box on the table. "Why don't you read it aloud? My voice is leaving me."

"Of course," said Tobias. While candlelight created shadows on the wall and the Mansion began to settle down for the night, Tobias read:

"March 17, 1790

"Give me leave, my dear General, to present you with a picture of the Bastille, just as it looked a few days after I had ordered its demolition—with the Main Key of that fortress of despotism. It is a tribute which I owe as a son to my Adoptive father, as an aide de camp to my General, as a Missionary of liberty to its Patriarch."

The two men sat in silence as they thought about the meaning of this letter. For one, it was a tribute to all he and his men fought for through years of hardship, intense and bloody battles, standing at the edge of despair, always with courage, determination, and belief in their cause. For the other, it was confirmation of his own beliefs. Although Tobias had not taken part in the battle, he had come to understand its importance and the courage of those who had. His years of work with this most exceptional of men had left its mark.

George Washington

"Lafayette is still doing great things in France," said Washington. "He is a fine man. I hope to see him again one day."

"Sir, did you say you saw Hamilton as well today?"

"Yes, yes, I did. He too was there at Yorktown. Along with Lafayette, he led a successful assault that certainly helped win the battle. He is brilliant but often believes he can't be wrong. The officers called him the Little Lion."

"Does he believe that slavery should be ended?" Tobias inquired.

"Yes, he does," replied Washington, taking a sip of the warm whiskey that Frank had provided. "He belongs to an abolitionist society, but he also believes in the property rights of slaveholders. Those positions are hard to reconcile. I have wrestled with them as well. Not only do I pray for abolition, for the sake of human dignity, I can clearly foresee that nothing but the rooting out of slavery can guarantee the continued existence of our union, by consolidating it in a common bond of principle. In the days ahead, I think, the Little Lion and Lafayette will understand how they influenced me. Laurens will too, from whatever heavenly spot he occupies.

"We will leave it at that," he said, wrapping Martha's shawl tighter as he rose. His cough had intensified. Taking a candle, he entered the hall, stopping for a moment to look at the Key to the Bastille. He glided his hand across the top of the display case and thought of all that had transpired to bring this key to his beloved home. "I always had a confident trust that we would not be ignored by heaven," he thought. "My trust was not misplaced."

As a strong bout of coughing engulfed him again, he put his hand on the wall to steady himself. His cough had blown out his candle and he stumbled up the steps in the dark.

William Lee

64   *George Washington*

Chapter Six

STONES IN MY HEART

Friday
December 13, 1799

11 a.m.

    William was awakened as usual that morning by the sounds of others rising to face their assigned tasks. There would be extra work this week, as Christmas was just twelve days away and the plantation was getting ready for days of feasting. This would mean an especially heavy load for Lucy in the cook house as she prepared for the many expected guests. While the other men went about preparing for the day, William stayed in his bunk and listened to their chatter. There was no need for him to hurry. The General did not demand as much from him as from the others. After his conversation with Christopher the day before, sleep had been elusive. What little sleep did come was filled with memories he had long since buried: the sight of his mother as she was sold, the sound of the whip as it cracked across the back of a young friend, the endless clang of the bell calling the slaves to work, the wailing of a young mother on her way to the auction block as her baby was taken from her arms, the cries of hungry young children.

When the others left, he finally was able to bury those images once more and rose to make ready for the day. He would not bother Lucy for breakfast today but took part of the rations offered to the others. He needed to go to the stable. It was where he did his best thinking.

The coat the General had given him during the war was tattered now, but it still provided warmth and protection. He also had his boots from the war, always shined, the way the General taught him. He limped out into the cold, crutches in hand, head bent against the falling snow, down the South Lane past the smokehouse filled with butchered hogs. An especially fine smoked ham would soon be taken down from the shelf to be part of Christmas dinner.

He passed the wash house next door as it emitted steam from within, a good place to be on this cold day. Slaves were continuously busy here as they performed the arduous task of carrying thirty buckets of water from the well and then bringing the water to a boil over a wood fire. The clothes and linens of the family and their guests were soaked, beaten, scrubbed, then hung to dry on racks. Next they were pressed with irons that had been heated in the fire. Most days, William Lee would pay a quick visit to Vina and Dolsey, slaves who did most of this never-ending work. Today he did not. He needed to get to the barn. His dreams from the night before were still with him.

As he approached the stable, he was once more impressed with its size and quality. The original wood frame building had burned down several years ago, giving the master a reason to put up a more substantial structure made of brick. It was a hub of activity, housing twenty-five horses and all the equipment needed for their care. Fifty-five prize mules were tethered in an attached shed.

As William entered the building, its familiar smells and sounds brought immediate comfort. The scent of horse sweat, manure, hay, and leather combined with the muted sounds of horses eating and snorting, donkeys braying, old leather saddles cracking, and the movement of horses against their stalls immediately calmed his distracted thoughts.

He opened the stall door to one of his favorite horses: a stallion of good quality and breeding, descended from the horse the General had provided for William during the war and very much like his ancestor: calm, responsive, and reliable. William sat down on an old stool in the corner. *What a gift God has given us in the horse,* he thought. His mind took him back to Yorktown, where his spyglass revealed the carcasses of four hundred horses floating in the York River. The memory of the fetid stench still nauseated him. That the British had purposely killed these creatures of God was a heinous crime.

"After the final battle when the light of day broke, I saw corpses all over the field, corpses from both sides," William recalled. "They were mainly black corpses. Slaves who had been promised their freedom by the British if they fought on their side. They were always used in the front lines. Some of those poor bastards were purposely exposed to smallpox and put in the forward lines in the hope they would be captured and infect our side. Many free black men who fought for the General lay dead as well, staring with unseeing eyes as vultures and hawks picked at their bones. The smell of death permeated the sandy soil and wafted across the battle scene, pushed by breezes from the sea. And there were numbers of other slaves promised their freedom by the British. But the British had not provided food, shelter, or medical care for them, and now they huddled in the woods nearby, close to death. They were just like the horses the British had slaughtered in the river.

"I was standing next to the General, waiting for orders, when I heard him say the terms of surrender would demand that all slaves who had joined the British with a promise of freedom would be returned to their owners. I did not stir, but stones clattered in my heart. I carry them still. I carry them still."

Other images that had long been dormant in the recesses of his brain surfaced in intermittent spurts: the British drummer boy waving the flag of surrender; British soldiers giving up their weapons by throwing them on the ground, hoping they would break; the sight of Washington riding Nelson through his troops to accept the surrender, and then about a week later accompanying the General on his ride to Eltham to find his stepson at death's door. The ride was a quiet one. William had provided for the General as best he could but he could not ease the pain of loss.

Remembering the battle scene, the dead horses, the broken promises of freedom, and his years of servitude, he stood and buried his face in the horse's neck, closed his eyes, breathed in the scent of sweat, grass, and salt air, and let the years of accumulated tears roll down his weathered face.

He took a deep breath, patted the horse's neck, and left the stable, hobbling through the snow on his crutches, ready to return to making shoes for his fellow slaves.

Chapter Seven

GRAVE CONCERN

Saturday
December 14, 1799

4 a.m.

As Washington made his way to the bedroom at the top of the stairs, his breathing became more labored. He found it difficult to remove his clothes and fell onto the bed coughing. For a fleeting second he thought of the dream he'd had a few days before: Martha fades and he is left alone. "Why does that keep recurring?" he asked himself. He was eventually able to sleep intermittently, but in the middle of the night, between two and three in the morning, he experienced a severe sore throat and shook Martha.

"I am not feeling well," he gasped as he tried to rise.

"Do not struggle, dear. Let me summon the doctor now."

"No, no, I will be all right. Just adjust my pillow a bit higher. I think that will help. I will be fine. I don't want you catching cold as well. I have suffered worse than this."

"But George, you sound awful."

William Lee   69

"No, no, we shall wait until Caroline comes to stoke the fire. I might be well by then. No sense disturbing people for nothing."

The two lay trying to sleep, but by five o'clock when Caroline came to stir the fire and provide warm water for washing, it was more than obvious that they needed medical help.

"Caroline," said Martha, "please find Mr. Lear and tell him to come at once. But first help me to get into my clothes. He should not see me in my nightdress."

Caroline found Martha's clothes from the day before and brought them to her. "Will these be all right, ma'am?"

"Yes, yes, anything, but be quick. Can't you hear the General struggling?"

"Yes, ma'am," she said, buttoning her mistress's dress. "I will run right away."

As the plantation came to life in the early morning light, Caroline flew down the back stairs, through the back door to the snow-covered walkway, and on to the cookhouse. Lucy was already there beginning her long day of producing meals.

"Where is Mr. Lear?" Caroline asked, catching her breath. "The General is sick and Mrs. Washington wants me to bring him quickly."

"I am not sure," Lucy answered. "He probably stayed the night because of the snow. I know he was up late with the General. Frank said they were still in the parlor long after he cleaned up. Check the guest room upstairs, the one next to Nelly and the baby. I will find Christopher and send him as well."

Returning to the second floor, Caroline knocked on the guest room door but there was no response. Knocking harder, she called out, "Mr. Lear, Mr. Lear, Mrs. Washington has sent me. She needs you right now."

Several minutes later a disheveled Tobias opened the door.

"What is the trouble?"

"It's the General, sir. He is sick and having a heap of trouble breathing. Mrs. Washington wants you to come."

"Yes, yes," Tobias answered. "I will be there at once." It must be serious, he thought. The General would not have allowed anyone to be disturbed unless he too felt it was serious.

While Tobias dressed, Caroline took a quick peek at the baby girl who lay with her mother in the room next door. She had been assigned to help the new mother. All looked well. She would return later.

As food smells wafted from the cookhouse, the slaves began their daily tasks, and the plantation animals announced the day in their own particular language, Caroline and Tobias ran down the front stairs and up the back stairs to the bedroom where Washington lay.

Not pausing to knock, Tobias ran in and found Washington having a difficult time breathing and scarcely able to utter a word intelligibly.

"Thank God you are here, Tobias," said Martha. "He is struggling so."

"Have you sent for the medicine we usually use for coughs and such?"

Caroline answered, "I will go to Lucy and get it, ma'am. She knows how it is made."

Once more Caroline ran to the cookhouse. By this time several of the kitchen workers had heard the news and watched with silent concern as Caroline helped Lucy find the ingredients.

"We need molasses, vinegar, and butter," said Lucy, "all mixed well. It takes a bit of stirring to make it blend."

As Lucy poured the ingredients together, Caroline stood by the big kitchen fireplace and warmed herself, if only for a brief minute.

Nathan, Lucy's helper, asked, "So what is wrong with the Master?"

"He is having trouble breathing and he's coughing heavily."

Frank, who had just come in, said, "He was coughing last night but did not seem to be uncomfortable. Master Lear tried to get him to take something. But he refused."

"Well, this looks ready now," said Lucy. "Hurry, Caroline. Tell him to drink it slowly."

As Caroline retraced her steps, Sweetlips sensed that the daily routine had been upset and quietly followed her up the back stairs to the bedroom.

"Sweetlips, you cannot come in," she said as they arrived at the bedroom door. "You know the mistress does not like hounds in the house. Just lie in the hall quietly; maybe she won't see you."

Entering the room, she saw that Christopher had arrived and had carried his master to a chair by the fire, hoping that the upright position might make it easier to breathe.

Caroline handed the medicine to Christopher, who gave some to the General. But when he attempted to swallow even a few tablespoons, he began to choke, almost to the point of convulsion.

Finding it hard to watch, Tobias told them to stop. Then he directed Christopher to send someone to Alexandria for the Washingtons' longtime friend and family doctor, James Craik.

As the small group watched helplessly, the General whispered, "Rawlins. Get him to bleed me."

"Not Rawlins," said Martha. "He is not a physician. He is only an overseer. What does he know? He has only given medicine to slaves, not generals."

"Rawlins," the General repeated. "Now."

"I will find him. He is probably in his office," said Christopher as he ran from the room.

"I think we should also call on Dr. Brown," Martha said. "Tobias, send someone for him."

"Yes, ma'am," said Tobias and hurriedly left the room, passing Rawlins and Christopher on the stairs.

"I am afraid the General is in a bad way, Rawlins," Tobias said. "I hope you can help him. Hurry."

Rawlins entered the room to find the General struggling, unable to swallow, even his own saliva. The overseer quailed at the thought of bleeding him.

The General looked at Rawlins and said, gently but firmly, "Don't be afraid."

With trembling hands Rawlins rolled up the General's sleeve, took a deep breath, and sliced into the skin, causing blood to run freely.

"The opening is not big enough," the General whispered.

"Oh, please, please. No more," Martha begged. "It is enough. Enough!"

"More, more," the General insisted.

When a pint of blood had been taken, Rawlins closed the wound and bandaged it. Then he wrapped the General's throat with flannel and soaked his feet in warm water. But the General continued to move about, trying to find a position that would make breathing easier. He never complained, maintaining the same poise and self-control he had displayed in other crises, whether war or politics or family deaths.

The morning light now filled the bedroom and did not seem to understand that this most remarkable man was gravely ill. The sound of hoof beats on the driveway leading to the Mansion announced the arrival of Dr. Craik. Led by Tobias to the back stairs, he climbed quickly and entered the bedroom, breathing heavily.

At the bedside, he took his friend's hand. "What is going on here?" he asked.

Washington turned and, grasping Dr. Craik's hand, gasped, "Can't swallow."

"How long has this been the case?" asked Dr. Craik.

"Since early this morning," said Martha. "He did not feel well last night, but as you know, he has always believed that his body will take care of him."

"I see he has been bled. How much?"

"A pint," answered Tobias.

"Please don't do that again," said Martha. "I don't think it will help. It will only weaken him more."

"I am convinced it is what needs to be done," said Dr. Craik as he put his arm around Martha's shoulder. "However, we will try something else first." Turning to Caroline, he said, "Could you bring us a teapot filled with sage tea, vinegar, and hot water?"

"Yes, sir," she said. "Right away." As Caroline entered the busy kitchen, Lucy asked, "How is the master? Did the molasses work?"

"Not at all," said Caroline. "It made him choke badly. They had to stop. It does not look good, Lucy."

They were concerned both for the General and for themselves.

The death of a master was life changing for his slaves. Would they be sold? Would their families be split apart? They looked at each with grave concern.

"Dr. Craik wants sage tea, vinegar, and hot water in a teapot. Quickly," said Caroline.

"Yes, yes, Caroline. It will only take a minute."

"Lucy, I think we must pray. The General is struggling so," said Caroline, "and they have already bled him."

"Yes, we will pray," said Lucy, taking Caroline's hand. With bowed heads they asked God to help their master and they prayed for their own future.

Lucy then scurried around the kitchen looking for the ingredients Dr. Craik had requested. "Here. Take the sage tea. I will send a tray for those who have not had anything to eat this morning."

Once again Caroline climbed the stairs and quickly entered the bedroom.

"Thank you," said Dr. Craik, as he came forward and took the teapot. "We must move him to the bed."

"Yes, sir," said Christopher, as he gently moved his master from the chair and laid him in the bed, propping pillows under him to elevate his chest.

"Here, now, my good friend," said Dr. Craik. "I want you to inhale the steam and try to get it into your lungs."

Washington nodded that he understood, but when he put his head back to inhale, he sounded as though he was suffocating. Everyone in the room watched with great concern.

"Martha," said Dr. Craik, "I am afraid this is very serious. I know you are opposed, but we need to bleed him again. It is

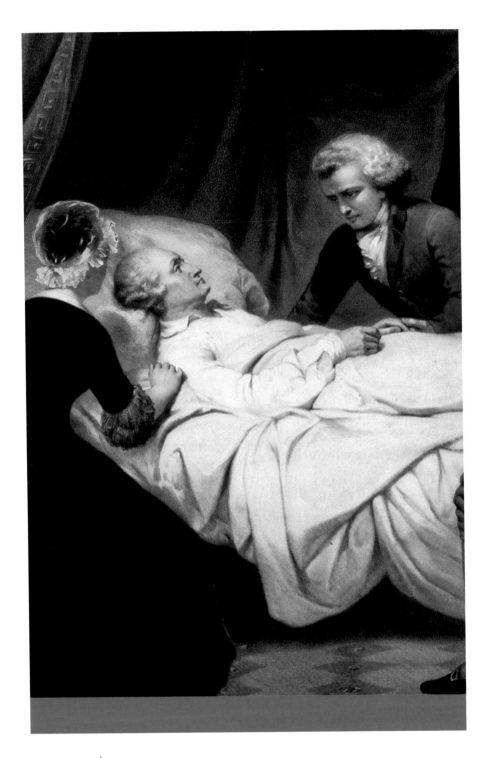

the only way. And I want to send for Dr. Elisha Dick and in Alexandria. He is a good man. Studied under Benjamin Rush. He may have other suggestions."

"Yes, yes, James. I understand," said Martha. "I am happy to have anyone who can help. Christopher, send someone to Alexandria for Dr. Dick, but before you go, put some more wood on the fire. And Caroline, I think you should check on Nelly and the baby. Don't mention just yet that her grandfather is sick."

"Yes, ma'am," said Caroline and left just as Molly arrived with the tray from Lucy. She passed the food around to those who had been in constant attendance all morning.

Tobias pulled a chair close to his great friend and patron and held his hand. The General's breathing was labored and he continued to gag when trying to swallow, causing him to drool.

As the clock in the hall ticked slowly on, there was a strange and ominous quiet around the Mansion and the outbuildings. The word had reached the slaves that the master was struggling and they knew that their future and their families' future hung in the balance.

When Dr. Dick and Dr. Brown arrived, Tobias took them to the General's bedside.

"How long has he been like this?" Dr. Dick asked.

"Since early this morning," said Martha. "He woke me and he was having a hard time breathing."

"He has been bled several times. We have also tried molasses with vinegar and inhaling steam from sage tea," said Dr. Craik. "He could not tolerate either one. I have known him for a very long time and I have seen him ill, but never like this."

"Have you considered an enema?" asked Dr. Dick.

"I have not. I think it would make him too uncomfortable."

"I think we should give it a try," said Dr. Dick. "Could we get some water and clean sheets?"

As Dr. Craik had feared, the procedure caused great discomfort. It also reduced Washington's body fluids even further.

"How much blood has been taken altogether?" asked Dr. Brown.

"Five pints," answered Dr. Craik.

"Oh, no," said Martha, "that is far too much. No more. No more."

"There is a new procedure," said Dr. Dick. "It is called a tracheotomy. A hole is punched in the trachea—the windpipe—and would help him to breathe."

"I've heard it is very risky," said Dr. Craik.

"Yes," Dr. Brown agreed. "I don't think he could tolerate it."

While the doctors were conferring there was a small knock at the door. There, disheveled, with tear-stained cheeks, stood Nelly.

"I heard the servants whispering that Grandpapa was sick so I came right away. What is wrong, Grandmother?"

"He is having a great deal of trouble breathing, Nelly. The doctors have tried many things but nothing seems to help."

Nelly quickly approached her step grandfather's bedside. Taking his hand, she said, "Oh, dear Grandpapa. You must fight this, just like you fought on the battlefield. You are strong. You must fight for all of us," she whispered, "even the new baby."

Washington, unable to speak, took her hand, squeezed it, and attempted a smile.

Tobias came to her side and put a hand on her shoulder.

Silence prevailed for several minutes.

"Nelly," said Martha, "you can help us all by saying some prayers.

You are not well enough to stay here with Grandpapa. You must look after yourself and your baby."

"Oh, but Grandmother. Just the other night he was dancing while I played his favorite music. What happened?"

"We don't know, my dear. It all came on quickly. But you must go to your little one and we will keep you informed. Caroline will go with you for a while."

"No, no. You need her here. I will be all right. I will be strong like Grandpapa," Nelly said as she kissed her grandmother and her dear grandpapa. "Please call me if you need some help."

The clock in the front hall chimed 3:30. Washington had been struggling all day and had not shown any sign of improvement. Turning to Martha, he said, "Go down to my study and bring the pair of wills that are in my desk drawer."

As Martha left the room, Christopher approached his master's bed and brushed his hair in the usual manner, straightened his sheets, and fluffed his pillow.

"Sit down, Christopher," said Washington. "You have been on your feet this whole time. Please take a seat."

It was about four o'clock when Martha came back from the study with the wills and gave them to her husband. He looked at them quickly and told her to throw the older one into the fire, indicating that the one written the previous July was the one he wanted.

"Yes, my dear old man," she said gently. "I understand." She crossed the room to the fireplace and dropped the first will into the flames, causing them to crackle as they consumed the paper.

Tobias took his place by the man who for so many years had guided him like a father, comforted him when his each of his young wives had died, encouraged and advised him, and treated him as a member of the family.

Washington now turned to him and, shifting restlessly, said in a deep hoarse voice, "I find that I am going; my breath cannot last long. I believed from the first that the disorder would prove fatal. Please arrange and record all my late military letters and papers. Settle my accounts and look over my books, and let Mr. Rawlins finish recording my other letters, which he has begun."

"Oh, but General, the end is not so close. You must fight like Nelly said."

Washington smiled and said, "I regard my death with perfect resignation, Tobias."

Dr. Brown and Dr. Dick left the room to discuss the situation while Dr. Craik stayed with his old friend.

Struggling for breath, Washington said, "Doctor, I die hard, but I am not afraid to go."

Tobias climbed into the bed beside the General and gently tried to turn him to help him find breath.

"I am afraid I shall fatigue you too much," said Washington.

"It is not hard," said Tobias. "I just want to make it a bit easier for you."

"Well, it is a debt we must pay to each other, and I hope that when you want aid of this kind you will find it."

Chapter Eight
THE SALUTE

Saturday
December 14, 1799
4:30 p.m.

William sat at his cobbler's table working on a field hand's shoe. These were the hardest to fix. They had been worn daily, trudging through sand, mud, snow, forest and fields. Made of inferior leather, without buckles, they did not last. William would do what he could, but he knew it would not be long before the shoe fell apart and someone would have to go without until the overseer found money to buy more.

It was nearing five o'clock; evening was fast approaching, still cold and wet. William noticed that the day was unusually quiet. Noises that accompanied work on the plantation were somehow subdued. When the door opened and Frank came in, William asked him, "What is happening? It has been so quiet today."

"Has no one told you, William? The General is very sick—not able to breathe. Caroline says he is struggling and experiencing

George Washington

much pain."

William dropped the shoe he was working on. He had seen the General in many dire situations, but never the kind Frank described.

"Has Dr. Craik come?" he asked.

"Yes, he is with him now."

"That's very good," said William. "Dr. Craik was with us all through the war. I know the General puts great faith in what he can do."

"I am not sure he can do anything at this point," said Frank. "Word is that they have tried molasses, sage tea, bleeding. Nothing seems to bring him relief. He can't breathe or even swallow. Caroline tells us it is gruesome to watch."

"I must go to him," said William. "I was close to him in the war. I was able to see what he needed before he even knew he needed it. Help me over to the Mansion, Frank. I don't want to slip in the snow."

Finding his tattered coat, William slipped into it and took the crutches Frank held for him. Together they left the slave barracks and turned toward the Mansion. It was winter-dark outside, and as William looked up toward the bedroom where his master lay, he could see candlelight flickering in the window and smell smoke coming from the chimney. In the distance he could hear hounds barking and donkeys braying from the stable area, all oblivious to what was happening in the big house.

He hobbled toward the back door and stood at the bottom of the stairs that led to the bedroom. With the help of Frank and all the strength he could muster, he slowly made his way up the steps. Sweetlips, who recognized him as an old friend, came forward with tail wagging but less enthusiastically than usual.

"Hello, my old friend," said William. "I see you are on guard, good soldier."

Answering Frank's knock, Christopher was surprised to see William.

"Sweetlips and I need to see the General," said William with some authority.

Christopher was startled but did not object. Since Mrs. Washington was not in the room at the moment, it would be all right for Sweetlips to enter. The hound went straight to Washington's bedside and licked his hand, seeming to encourage him not to give up.

"Under the bed," said Washington. "Quickly. The lady will be back soon."

"General, sir, I am here," said William. "Right close by. I see you need a little tending to. Molly, could you bring a warm cloth so I can wash face and pull back his hair?"

Washington smiled as he heard William's voice and extended his hand.

William stood straight and saluted. Washington returned the salute and William took his hand. There was not a dry eye in the room as enslaved and free watched two men who for different reasons had depended on each other, two men who had found mutual respect in a world where that rarely happened between master and slave. Deep and lasting friendships are forged on battlefields, and this one was strengthened again and again, through setbacks and discouragement.

"William, I do die hard, but I feel I am nearing the end." he gasped.

William washed the General's face and gently dried it. He combed his hair, straightened the sheets, and plumped the pillows. As night settled in, a respectful quiet filled the room, broken only by the crackling fire and the wind blowing around the corners of the Mansion. Gentle tears ran down William's face as he once more saluted his General.

Frank came forward and, handing him his crutches, said, "William, I think it best that we go now. It is time."

The two men descended the stairs and walked slowly into the dark, cold night.

Chapter Nine

'TIS WELL

Saturday
December 14, 1799

5 p.m.

Between five and six o'clock, as night began to fill the dusk sky, Doctors Dick, Brown, and Craik approached the bedside. Dr. Craik asked the General if he could sit up. He held out his hand and Tobias raised him up.

Looking at his doctors, Washington said, "I find myself going. I thank you for your attentions, but I pray you take no more trouble about me. Let me go off quietly. I cannot last long."

"All that we have done seems not to have had any effect," said Dr. Brown, speaking to Martha. "I think we should confer downstairs."

"Yes, please do," she replied. "I am hopeful you will find another suggestion. It is hard to watch him struggle so. It is as if he is slowly strangling. He is exhausted."

"May I get something for you, ma'am?" asked Molly.

"No, no; I don't think I could eat now."

Dr. Brown and Dr. Dick left the room, but Dr. Craik sat with bowed head next to the fire, absorbed in quiet grief. Caroline, Molly, Christopher, and Charlotte stayed to help when needed.

About eight o'clock, the doctors returned and applied poultices to his legs and feet, without effect. The General still struggled painfully, gagging and searching for breath.

Two hours later, with great effort, Washington, clearly concerned about those around him, said in a low, broken voice, "I am just going. Have me decently buried, but do not let my body be put in the vault less than three days after I am dead."

Tobias nodded his head, unable to speak.

"Do you understand me?" asked Washington.

"Yes, sir," said Tobias, still holding his mentor's hand.

" 'Tis well."

It was between ten and eleven o'clock when the General took his hand from Tobias's and felt his own pulse. Then his hand dropped and his face took on a different expression. Dr. Craik came to his side and knew that his great, good friend had died without even a sigh. He closed the General's eyes and silently stood by him.

The room was filled with grief. Martha, sitting at the foot of the bed, asked in a firm and controlled voice, "Is he gone?"

Tobias, who still could not speak, held up his hand to indicate that the General had indeed died.

" 'Tis well," she said, as stoic as her husband had been. "All is now over. I shall soon follow him. I have no more trials to pass through."

Dr. Craik sent Molly downstairs to ask the doctors to come up and confirm the death. Christopher approached Tobias and said,

"The mistress wants you to take care of the things found in the General's pockets—keys and such."

"Yes," he answered, "I will wrap them in his handkerchief and keep them in my room."

When Molly brought Dr. Brown and Dr. Dick into the room, Sweetlips took the opportunity to quietly crawl from under the bed. With drooping ears and tail, the General's hound scurried dejectedly out of the room. She knew her master was no longer there. She did not need the doctors' confirmation.

Feeling for a pulse and a heartbeat, the doctors confirmed what everyone else in the room had witnessed. The great and good General Washington was indeed dead. The struggle was over.

Caroline quietly approached Martha and asked, "Should we toll the bell, ma'am?"

"Yes, I don't think we should wait until morning. Let William do it. Yes, he should do it. Christopher, you can go and tell him."

Christopher walked slowly from the room into the dark moonless night and went to the slave barracks. He found William in his bed, not asleep but in quiet contemplation.

"He is gone, William. The General is gone. The mistress wants you to toll the bell."

William sat up and said, "It would be an honor. One last thing I can do for him. You might have to help me get there."

"Be careful," said Christopher. "It is slippery out there."

"That won't stop me—I will toll the bell for General George Washington."

Chapter Ten

KEEPING WATCH

Sunday
December 15, 1799

12 a.m.

Martha was still sitting in silence by her partner of forty years when the door opened softly and Nelly came in with the baby.

"Oh, Grandmama, is he gone?"

"Yes, dear, I am afraid so."

Nelly came forward and embraced her grandmother.

" 'Tis well," said Martha. "He was suffering so."

"Oh, Grandmama, how will things go on without him?" she cried.

Martha squeezed her granddaughter's hand and said, "You know he wants us to carry on, but it will be hard."

Wiping away tears, Nelly said, "You come and sleep with the baby and me tonight. I don't want you to be alone."

"I will come soon," said Martha, "but now next steps must be taken. Now my very best friend must be given the care that will

make him ready for burial. We will have to get him downstairs so his body can be prepared."

"We will need six strong men," said Dr. Craik, "and I would like to be one of them."

"I can help," said Christopher, "and I will find Frank and Cyrus. We can get Adam as well."

"I can help too," said Tobias.

"I think that is all that can be done right now," said Nelly as she put her arm around her grandmother. "Come now. You need to rest."

Martha followed, too tired to protest.

Within half an hour, Christopher returned with Frank, Cyrus, and Adam. Dr. Craik and Tobias stood by the bed and helped gently lift the General's body with straps provided by Frank. They moved from the bedroom and down the hall, proceeding to struggle down the steps, with the body sometimes hitting the risers and making a muted thud. They took him to the New Room, lit now with several candles, and laid him on a table covered with blankets.

"I think we can do the basic work tonight," said Dr. Craik. "Tomorrow we can dress him for burial. Christopher, we will need warm water to bathe him. He struggled so much, he is covered with sweat. We must also pack all his orifices. If we don't, it will cause a stench. I will sew his mouth shut. And you can help me with his hair. We are all so exhausted from this day; that will be enough until tomorrow."

"Should I light the fire?" asked Frank.

"No, the cold will postpone decay. We can bear one more hour of cold for him."

While the snow continued to fall and the wind blew intermittently, six men who had had different relationships with this extraordinary man stood by his body to offer one last act of friendship and tribute. Some relationships were between slave and master, some as mentor, some as loyal friends. Each had seen the courage, simplicity, quiet dignity, and concern for others, as well as the occasional flare of temper and the exacting expectations.

Now as William tolled the Mansion bell, they stood together in the General's favorite room realizing that this man, who had changed the world, was gone and could not be replaced.

When they had finished preparing his body as best they could, they each left to find rest for the night, Dr. Craik and Tobias in Mansion bedrooms, the four slaves in their barracks.

When all had departed and the house had found lonely quiet, the door to the New Room opened and William Lee entered with Sweetlips at his heels. "I will take the watch," he said to himself, "just like I did during the war." He approached the body, once more saluted his commander, and pulled a chair close to his side. Candles in the room made shadows on the wall and lit the faces of the two men who had held each other in mutual respect. Sweetlips lay next to William, companions in grief. They stayed there until the house awakened early the next morning, when William left quietly and headed toward the slave barracks.

Chapter Eleven

FACING DEATH'S REALITY

Sunday
December 15, 1799
4 a.m.

Lucy rose earlier than normal. She would have much to do in the kitchen. She tried not to think about what lay ahead for her and her family. They could be sold and separated to who knows where. She kept those thoughts at bay as she entered the cookhouse. Relatives would be arriving and they would need to be fed. She would also have to begin the meal that would be served after the funeral. And now Christmas was ten days away. She was not sure what the mistress would want.

Caroline also rose early. She and Molly had not left their master's bedroom when the others had departed with his body, staying behind to clean what they could. They opened windows so that the smells of sage, tobacco, blood, excrement, sweat, molasses, and vinegar would escape into the night air. They stripped the bed, flipped the mattress, and put on clean sheets, swept the hearth, provided new candles, and emptied the chamber pot.

When they had finished, Caroline ran from the Mansion to the slave cabin she and Peter and their six children occupied. Peter was asleep when she entered but she shook him awake.

"Peter, Peter did you hear? The master has died. What will happen to us?" she cried. "What about the children? Will they sell them? Will they sell us?"

Peter rose and took his wife in his arms. He could not answer her questions or calm her fears. He had the same concerns, concerns that had followed them their entire life.

"We have to be strong," he said to Caroline. "We have some time before those decisions are made. Right now we cannot let fear overwhelm us. We must carry on as usual, but we must be alert to any changes."

"Oh, Peter, maybe we should just run now. They will be busy with all the preparations. We could just slip away."

"We can't just 'slip away' with six children," said Peter. "Besides, they would notice right away because they will want me to prepare the General's horse and get the barn ready for the guests' carriages and horses. And if we did run and got caught, they would certainly sell us all without hesitation."

Caroline knew he was right, but his words did not stop the tears from flowing. Tears not for her master but for being his slave, with no control over her life. She collapsed on the bed and tried to make the future disappear.

William Lee passed other slaves as he left the Mansion that morning and hobbled back to the slave barracks. He was tired from his long vigil and he was tired by grief. He sat on the side of his bed trying to take in what had happened in just a few days. Other men in the barracks kept asking him questions: What would happen now? Did he know anything? Did the General ever say?

"No," William replied, "he never said. I only know that the time I spent with him, whether at a foxhunt, in battle, or just helping him get dressed, he always showed concern for others. He was an honest and stand-up man. I wish I could answer your concerns, but I cannot. And right now all I want to do is sleep. If somehow I find out anything, I promise to tell you," he said as he put his head on the pillow and pulled up his blanket.

Tobias Lear rose early as well and entered the small dining room as the breakfast bell rang at the normal hour of seven. Mrs. Washington and Nelly were already there. Still the organizer, still able to carry on as she had done through the many trials in her life, and still concerned about others, Martha said, "You must be hungry. You ate almost nothing yesterday. Sit down now."

Tobias took his chair as Frank came forward with a hearty meal. All were silent for a while. It was hard to accept that their General was gone.

"Now, Tobias, today I want you to send someone up to Alexandria to have a coffin made," said Martha. "You must ask the doctor to get the right measurements. We will need black crepe to hang in the windows and some black material for scarves; black ribbon as well. Don't forget the mourning clothes for the servants and for the family. I think Christopher can help you with that. Speaking of Christopher, he should have a new pair of shoes. Cyrus needs them as well. William Lee should be able to do that in time. I am sure I can put you in charge. Right now Nelly and I must go and talk with Lucy about food. There will be many people here and we must be prepared."

On their way out, the two women encountered Dr. Craik, who put his arm around Martha's shoulders. They had been friends for many, many years.

"Oh, James, I know you tried so hard to save him."

"We will miss him so," said Dr. Craik with tears in his eyes. "He was a dear friend and true."

Squeezing his hand, Martha said, "We must carry on now. There will be many people coming. Thank you, James."

After the doctor had eaten, he went to the New Room with Tobias where the body lay. Dr. Craik took the measurements.

1. Six feet, three and one-half inches in length
2. 1 foot, nine inches across the shoulders
3. Two feet across the elbows.

When Christopher arrived to help, Tobias said, "Mrs. Washington wants you to send Cyrus to Alexandria to the Ingle brothers and have the coffin made according to the measurements. It should be made of mahogany and lined with an inner lead coffin."

"Yes, sir, right away," said Christopher.

Turning toward the doctor, Tobias said, "I think we should wait until the last of the week for burial so that relatives will have time to get here."

"I am afraid we can't wait that long," replied Dr. Craik. "We are not exactly sure what caused his death; whatever it was may be communicable. Keeping the body that long could cause trouble."

"I think then that Wednesday the eighteenth at noon would

closely correspond with what the General desired," said Tobias. "I will inform Mrs. Washington and I am quite sure she will agree."

Still bereft and drained, Tobias went to the General's study to compose letters telling President John Adams, Alexander Hamilton, and the General's nephew Bushrod Washington, among others, of the great loss. With each letter he finished, the great man's death became more of a reality.

Chapter Twelve
GETTING READY

Monday
December 16, 1799

5 a.m.

As weak winter sunlight fell upon the plantation, life seemed to continue as normal. Animals had to be fed; people, both enslaved and free, had to eat as well. The stable and barn had to be cleaned and ready for guests' horses and their coaches. The Mansion must be swept and dusted from top to bottom, bed sheets changed, cots made up, rooms aired. The slaves who accomplished this work were tense and worried about what the future held for them, but they worked on.

Tobias rose early again, breakfasted, and headed toward the family tomb with Christopher. It was not far, just past the stables at the end of the South Lane. Still covered in snow, it sparkled in the sun. The sound of donkeys braying traveled from the barn and met with a slight wind that gently wrapped itself around trees and people.

George Washington

"I have not been here in quite some time," Tobias said to Christopher. "It is easy to ignore. I suppose it seems easier to accommodate death if you ignore it." Inspecting the vault, he continued, "This must be opened and all this trash cleaned up. We have to make everything decent. The General was always aware of appearances."

"I understand, sir," said Christopher.

"Mrs. Washington would like to have a new door," said Tobias.

"Yes, sir," said Christopher, as he considered who would have any kind of time to accomplish the tasks. "We will get started right away, sir."

Assured that Christopher would carry out the tasks, Tobias headed back to the Mansion, where he was informed that the militia of the Freemasons in Alexandria was determined to show their respect by attending the body to the grave.

"There are so many of them," he thought out loud and went out the back door through the passage to the cookhouse.

"Lucy, I think our numbers are greatly increasing," he called over the din of food being prepared for meals and the funeral reception. "Is Frank here?"

"Yes, sir," said Lucy. "Just there in the pantry."

"Good morning, Frank," said Tobias. "Looks like we are going to need more food than normal."

"Yes, sir. The distillery has already sent twenty-nine gallons of whiskey, and we have ten gallons in storage from Mr. Gilpin. Mrs. Washington has ordered forty pounds of cake and three large wheels of cheese. She has been working all day in preparation, and the rest of us are trying to help."

"I knew I could depend on you, Frank," said Tobias. "Please let me know if you run into any problems."

"Yes, sir," replied Frank.

When Tobias left, Frank thought, "The problem, if you really want to know, is that we are all worried about the future and where we will be. Here at Mount Vernon or in some other plantation far away? And the children—where will they be?" He tried to steady his hands and set the table for dinner, while his thoughts ran through all manner of possibilities.

Chapter Thirteen

RIGHT BY HIS SIDE

Tuesday
December 17, 1799

1 p.m.

Word of President Washington's death spread quickly in the neighborhood and across the fledgling country. Everyone felt the loss of this great man even if they were not personally close to him. Newspapers were bordered in black, naval vessels flew their colors at half-mast, businesses closed, and bells tolled across the nation. People understood the many sacrifices he had made and the great part he had played in the founding of the nation.

At Mount Vernon, preparations continued across the plantation. Around one o'clock, Tobias met the coffin that had been made in Alexandria. Lined in lead and quite heavy, it was difficult to unload. Several slaves who had been called to help struggled through the slushy snow and carried it into the house.

"Please follow me," Tobias said. "We will put it in the New Room where the body lies." As he led the way through the front door and down the hall, those at work in the Mansion stopped what they were doing out of respect for their master.

"You can put the coffin right there," Tobias said, pointing to a table under the great windows. When the coffin was settled, Tobias inspected it to see if it was made to the right specifications.

"Yes, I see you have lined it with black lace, as requested. The silver plate is beautiful. Let me just check the wording."

General

George Washington

Departed this life on the 14th of December

1799, Aet. 68

"It is well done, engraved by a master, and the inscriptions on the lid, beautiful." Tobias read aloud as he gently touched the flowing words:

Surge Ad Judicium

Gloria Deo

Turning to the men from Alexandria who had delivered the coffin, Tobias said, "I must detain you a bit longer so we can make sure the measurements are correct, and I must send for a few people to help us move the body."

Seeing Christopher outside, he called to him and asked him to find Cyrus and Frank.

When all were assembled, they wrapped the cold and graying body in the burial shroud that was provided and gently placed the General in his coffin.

"It fits as measured," said Tobias. "I wish he could rise up and tell us it is very comfortable. Oh, how I wish this were a bad dream. I think you can go now," he said to the men from

Alexandria. "You have done all that was required." Turning to Christopher, Frank, and Cyrus, he said, "But we have much more to do."

"Yes, sir, I know," said Christopher. "I will wash his face one last time and comb his hair."

"I would like to cut a bit of it," said Tobias. "I think some of the family might like to have it to put in a locket."

"I will do that," said Christopher. "I have combed and cut his hair often and I can do it for the last time." He stepped forward and snipped several pieces, wrapped them in paper, and gave them to Tobias.

"Thank you," said Tobias. "It is all we will be able to keep of him."

"Is there anything else, sir?" Christopher asked. "I must go to William Lee and see if the new shoes are ready."

"That will be fine," answered Tobias.

Christopher left the Mansion and hurried through the snow to William's workshop. He found him working hard on the last shoe.

"William," he said, "who would have thought last week when we were talking about our place in this world that the master would soon be dead?"

"I was thinking the same thing," said William as he tapped away at the sole. "It is a great loss to me. I can't say that a master could ever be a true friend, but I know I respected him and I think he came to respect me."

Christopher was silent. In the past three days he had stood by his dying master and helped in every way possible. He had helped give him medicine, carried him to a chair, washed his face and body, watched as he was bled, carried his dead body downstairs, washed it, cut his hair, dressed him in a shroud, and helped place him in a coffin. He knew the General well and would miss him, but he was a young man, only twenty-four, who yearned for freedom, the kind of freedom his master had fought for, but not for those of color. He looked at William and knew that there was not much else to say.

"The shoes are finished now," said William. "They even have buckles. You will look fine for the master's funeral. Go along now. There is much to do."

"Thanks, William. I was able to get this for you," said Christopher as he handed William a lock of the General's hair.

"Thank you," said William as he took the gift from Christopher. "I took care of this hair for more years than I can count," he said, choking back tears.

"Where will you be tomorrow?" asked Christopher.

"Right by his side, just like during the war. I will see him to his grave too."

Christopher put his hand on William's shoulder and quietly left the cobbler's shop.

Chapter Fourteen

TIME TO SAY GOODBYE

Wednesday
December 18, 1799

As dawn broke, a flurry of respectfully quiet activity was taking place around the Mansion: food prepared and served, more food prepared for after the burial, horses boarded and coaches cared for, fires laid, beds made, and snow shoveled.

Around ten o'clock, Tobias ordered that the coffin be brought to the Piazza at the east side of the house within view of the Potomac River, so loved by Washington. It was placed on a bier and kept open so that the guests could view the remains.

Since the funeral was set for noon, many friends and relatives began to arrive about eleven. They took the opportunity to view the General's body one last time and then conversed quietly about the cause of death and the great void it left.

Frank approached Tobias and said, "I have received word, sir, that the militia is having trouble getting here but hope to arrive by three."

"I am not surprised that they are late. It is a lot of people to organize. I should think, though, that if the General could speak, he would admonish them. He was so punctual in everything. We will have to offer some food to those who are already here. Do you think Lucy can take care of that?"

"Yes, sir, she is quite ready. I will get some others to help."

By 2:30 most of the Freemasons militia had arrived and the funeral procession began to assemble. It left the house led by the cavalry, followed by the infantry and the guard. A band played a dirge accompanied by muffled drums. From the Potomac an anchored schooner began firing a thirteen-gun salute. The sound echoed across the surrounding hills and valleys. Then came clergy. Cyrus and Wilson, slaves attired in full mourning dress, led Washington's riderless horse that carried his saddle, holster, and pistols. His well-polished boots were reversed in the stirrups, the sign of a fallen soldier who would never ride again. Peter Hardiman had worked well into the night grooming the horse and making sure all his tack was polished. It sparkled now in the winter sun.

The General's coffin on its bier followed, protected by the militia and honorary pallbearers. Next came very old and good friends, among whom were Dr. Craik and Tobias.

Tobias whispered to Dr. Craik, "Where are Mrs. Washington and Nelly?"

"I don't think they will attend," said Dr. Craik. "It is very difficult for them, in so many ways. I fully understand. I would not be surprised if they are watching from an upstairs window."

As the procession made its way toward the family vault, other mourners fell in line, among them William Lee, dressed in his coat from the Revolution and hobbling on his crutches. Other slaves left their work to join in the tribute to their master, trying not to think about what might come next.

Outside the vault, a clergyman read the order of burial from the Episcopal Book of Common Prayer and Dr. Dick performed the rituals of the Freemasons. As the coffin was moved into the vault, the sounds of eleven cannon being fired into the air and infantry muskets being discharged surrounded the mourners. For all in attendance, it was profoundly moving. This special man, not consumed by power, who had a shared sense of humanity and freedom was gone. There would never be another like him.

When the new vault door was closed and locked, Tobias turned to those present and said, "Mrs. Washington would like you to come for food and drink in the New Room before you take your leave. You are most welcome. Frank will show you the way."

Upon entering the New Room, the mourners found a table full of meats, fish, salads, cheeses, fruit, and a variety of desserts, prepared by the slaves who now stood ready to meet the needs of the mourners. The guests stayed longer than expected. Their hearts told them that when they left, Mount Vernon would never be the same again.

Chapter Fifteen

A QUESTIONABLE FUTURE

Thursday
December 19, 1799
10 a.m.

Grief hovered over the Mansion and its inhabitants. They were all trying to cope, as General Washington wished, yet they knew that grief would be a lasting companion. They knew they would see him in all the familiar places and hear his voice.

Tobias, who had gone home the night before, returned around ten to the Mansion, where he found Martha in the small parlor.

"Good morning, Mrs. Washington."

"Good morning, Tobias. I hope you found some rest. I know you have been very busy these past few days, and I want you to know that I appreciate your help."

"Yes, ma'am," Tobias replied. "I did tell the General that I would take care of his papers. Do you feel up to talking about them today?"

"Oh, Tobias." She sighed. "I don't know when I will feel up to it, if ever."

"Quite understandable," said Tobias.

There was respectful silence for a few minutes and then Martha said, "I think I can promise you that the day after Christmas we can look at the papers. In the meantime, perhaps you could arrange them in order of importance. Would that be all right with you?"

"Yes, ma'am."

"I suppose," said Martha, "that if I busy myself with Christmas, I can soften some of my thoughts. And also, Tobias, you know I have been sleeping with Nelly and the baby these past few nights. I have decided that I will move to the bedroom on the third floor. I just cannot go back to the room that George and I shared for so many years. Could you ask Christopher to see that the attic room is made ready and my things are moved?"

"Yes, ma'am, I will talk with Christopher this morning," Tobias said.

"Thank you," said Martha. "And now, even though I don't feel like celebrating, I must go talk with Lucy about Christmas preparations."

Strong, disciplined, and self-aware, she knew she could not control death, but she could still control the kitchen and Christmas. As she approached the cookhouse she could hear animated conversation coming from inside. It stopped when she opened the door, and she heard the sounds of several people scurrying to leave through the back door.

"Good morning, Lucy," she said.

"Good morning, Ma'am," said Lucy, curtseying.

"I thought we should talk about Christmas," said Martha. "You know it is only six days away. But because of the circumstances, I don't feel the celebration has to be what we are used to. Have you started the preparations yet?"

"Why, yes, Ma'am," Lucy replied. "I have chosen the ham from the smokehouse, the plum pudding is mellowing, and we have candied the crabapples."

"I think we can skip the marzipan hedgehog and the Twelfth Night cake this year," said Martha. "But we can still have turkey and duck. I will consider the rest."

"How many guests do you think there will be?" Lucy asked.

"Oh, I have no idea," answered Martha. "Some of the close-by relatives might come, and maybe Dr. Craik and his family, and Tobias. I would say to prepare for twenty."

"Yes, ma'am," said Lucy.

"Are you all right, Lucy?" asked Martha. "You seem distracted."

"I am fine," she replied, not wanting to tell her newly widowed mistress all the things that were distracting her: Would her children be sold? Would she and Frank be sold? Who would take the General's place in overseeing the slaves? Would she still have the same job? Her concern and fear were shared across the five farms of the plantation.

Within six days, Christmas came once again to Mount Vernon. Martha did not attend the service at Christ Church in Alexandria as she normally did on the holiday. She dressed now in the somber black wool of mourning with a shawl of black lace around her shoulders, her hair covered with a white cap trimmed with black ribbon. A few relatives came to share Christmas dinner, the first without the General. Nelly and her husband, Lawrence, along with the baby, were there; Tobias came, as did Dr. Craik and his family.

Lucy and her helpers provided a lovely meal that brought warmth to the unusual quiet of the Christmas table.

When the meal was over and the guests began to disperse, Tobias reminded Martha that the next day would be a good time to look at the General's papers. She agreed and advised him to come around ten the next morning.

As she made her way up the stairs to the small room on the third floor that she had requested, she felt tired, flat, and filled with deep sorrow. She had buried four children, two husbands, her parents, all her brothers and sisters. It would be extremely difficult to accept the future.

Chapter Sixteen

WORK TO BE DONE

Thursday Morning
December 19, 1799

Morning broke as if to say with pride to the accompanying wind that there never would be another December 26, 1799. There was a clear sky with no signs of snow, but the temperature affirmed that winter was still around.

After breakfast Martha met Tobias in the Front Parlor. Frank had laid a fire for light and warmth. Tobias brought the important papers.

Initially they talked briefly about the few bills that should be paid. They discussed letters from people who did not know of the General's death. They should be answered quickly and given the news.

"Then there is the matter of the will," said Tobias. "It should be read in the presence of the executors. He has provided us with a list."

"Do we have to do it soon?" Martha asked.

"Yes, it would be best," said Tobias.

"And what executors has he named?"

"Last summer, July ninth, he wrote the will. His notes say the executors are you; his nephews William Augustine Washington, Bushrod Washington, George Steptoe Washington, Samuel Washington, and Lawrence Lewis; and his ward, your grandson George Washington Parke Custis, if he had turned twenty before the General's death."

"They are all good choices," said Martha. "Five of them served in the Continental Army. They will follow the wishes of their General."

"Should I notify them?" Tobias inquired.

"Yes. Do you think we could get them here by Monday?"

"If I can reach them quickly. I could send messengers today, and since most of them live in the area and are anxious to help, I am sure they will come. I will ask them to arrive by noon on Monday."

Martha left the parlor wishing that if she turned around and went back, her life partner would be sitting there with a cup of tea. She knew that was not to be, and grief engulfed her once more.

Chapter Seventeen

FULFILLING WISHES

Monday
December 30, 1799
12 p.m.

The breath of dawn had come slowly over the plantation on the second-last day of the century. It brought the promise of a bright and mild day, warm enough to turn the snow that had accumulated the week before into a muddy slush that found its way into the halls of the Mansion and impeded work in many areas of the property.

At noon, those whom George Washington had named as his executors began to make their way up the Mansion drive. Frank, dressed as usual in the red and white of the Washington livery, greeted each by name, sent their carriages to the stables, and showed them the way to the Front Parlor, where he announced their presence.

There were five men and one woman. George Washington

William Lee

In the name of God amen

I George Washington of Mount
Vernon a citi... of the United States,
and lately Pr...ident of the same,
do make, ord... and declare this
Instrument, ... h is written with
my own hand, ... d every page there
of subscribed ... h my name, to be
my last Will & ... tament, revo:
king all other ...

...primus All m... ...ots, of which there
are but few, a... none of magnitude
are to be punctu... ... and speedily paid
and the Legac... ...reinafter bequea... h
ed, are to be dis... ...rged as soon as cir
cumstances will ...rmit, and in the
manner directe...

...m. To my dear... ...oved wife Mar
tha Washington ... ...ir e and bequeath
the use, profit ... ... benefit of my whole
Estate, real and ... ...nal; for the term
of her natural li... except such parts
thereof as are ... ...ifically disposed
of hereafter ... ... lot in
the Town of Al...
Pitt & Cameron ...
her heirs for e...

George Washington

Parke Custis, the General's step grandson and ward, was not present because he was not yet twenty years of age as Washington had stipulated in his will. He was just eighteen.

Martha, always organized and aware of her guests' needs, had instructed Frank to make sure the ever popular Virginia punch would be on hand.

Frank had also laid a table with tea and small cakes for the group, built a fire, and provided tobacco for the comfort of those who now assembled in curious anticipation of the great man's last wishes.

Martha greeted the group with genuine warmth. She had known them, all of them her husband's nephews, since they were children.

They were a distinguished group, polished and educated, all landholders. William Augustine Washington, at forty-seven the oldest, had served as a cavalry officer in the Revolution. Bushrod Washington, thirty-seven, had served as a private. Lawrence Lewis, whose mother was Washington's sister, Betty, was thirty-two and married to Martha's granddaughter Nelly. He too had served as a young man in the Continental Army. The youngest were Samuel Washington, twenty-nine, and George Steptoe Washington, twenty-eight. All of these men had great respect for their uncle and were honored to be named as executors.

When all were seated and comfortable she addressed the group. "Who would like to read?"

"I would be honored," responded Lawrence Lewis.

"Thank you," said Martha as she handed the document to him and took a deep breath.

Lewis carefully laid the document on the table and, adjusting his glasses, read the title with a clear and strong voice.

> *In the name of God amen I George Washington of Mount Vernon,*
> *a citizen of the United States, and lately President of the same, do make,*
> *ordain and declare this instrument: which is written with my own hand and*
> *every page there of subscribed with my name to be my last will and testament*
> *revoking all others.*
>
> *Imprimus. All my debts, of which there are but few, and none of*
> *magnitude, are to be punctually and speedily paid—and the Legacies*
> *hereinafter bequeathed, are to be discharged as soon as circumstances will*
> *permit, and in the manner directed.*

Lewis took a sip of the tea Frank had provided and said, "He certainly had a clear hand. The document is not hard to decipher." He continued to read aloud:

> *Item. To my dearly beloved wife Martha Washington I give and bequeath*
> *the use, profit and benefit of my whole Estate, real and personal, for the term*
> *of her natural life—except such parts thereof as are specifically disposed of*
> *hereafter: My improved lot in the Town of Alexandria, situated on Pitt &*
> *Cameron streets, I give to her and her heirs forever; as I also do my household*
> *& Kitchen furniture of every sort & kind, with the liquors and groceries which*
> *may be on hand at the time of my decease; to be used & disposed of as she may*
> *think proper.*

Reading silently ahead, Lewis was unable to stifle the surprise the next lines occasioned. All were now listening intently—even Frank, who had been trained not to pay attention to the business discussions of his masters.

> *Item. Upon the decease of my wife, it is my Will & desire that all*
> *the Slaves which I hold in my own right, shall receive their freedom. To*
> *emancipate them during her life, would, tho' earnestly wished by me, be*

George Washington

household & Kitc... ...rniture of
every sort & kind, w... ...the liquors and
groceries which ma... be on hand at
the time of my dece...se; to be used &
disposed of as she m...y think proper.

... Upon the decease ...f my wife, it is
my Will & desire th... ...all the Slaves
which I hold in ... ...own right, shall
...receive their free... ...— To emanci...
...pate them durin... ...life, would, tho'
earnestly wish... ...me, be attended
with such insu... ...ble difficulties on
account of their ... ...xture by Mar...
...riages with the ... ...r Negroes, as to
excite the most pa... ...ful sensations,
if not disagreeabl... ...nsequences from
the latter, while ... ...scriptions are
in the occupancy ... the same Propri...
...etor; it not being ... my power under
the tenure by which ... e Dower Negros —
are held, to man... ...them. — And
whereas among ... e who will re=
...ceive freedom ac... ...ding to this de=
...vise, there may ... me, who from
old or bodily in... ...ties, and others
who on account... n infancy, that
...will be unable t... port themselves
it is ... ...re that all who
...f second descrip...
...ably cloathed &
...hey live; — and

attended with such insuperable difficulties on account of their intermixture by
Marriages with the dower Negroes, as to excite the most painful sensations, if
not disagreeable consequences from the latter, while both descriptions are in the
occupancy of the same Proprietor; it not being in my power, under the tenure
by which the Dower Negroes are held, to manumit them.

The words "All the slaves which I own in my own right shall receive their freedom" hung in the room for a moment. Then Bushrod shouted, "Huzzah! He actually did it. We had discussed it many times. I wanted to return slaves to Africa, Washington has gone further and freed them. Imagine!" He smiled. "Just imagine!"

"He discussed it with me several times," said Lewis, "but never told me he had actually put it in his will."

"Incredible. The country's first President frees his slaves. My uncle frees his slaves," whispered George Steptoe as he filled his pipe with tobacco. "This will be a matter of great concern in Virginia. Great concern! I foresee many consequences."

Martha was quiet offering no opinion.

Frank inhaled deeply and tried to pretend he had not heard, but when he brought tea around his hands began to shake. It was not fear now but unmitigated joy, joy, joy.

He had to restrain himself from running outside, ringing the bell, and telling the whole plantation. It was not immediate freedom, but freedom is what the future held.

After several minutes of absorbing what they just heard, Lewis said, looking over his spectacles, "We must continue. Let's see now. Where was I? Oh, yes, right here."

And whereas among those who will receive freedom according to this
devise, there may be some, who from old age or bodily infirmities, and others

who on account of their infancy, that will be unable to support themselves; it is my Will and desire that all who come under the first and second description shall be comfortably clothed and fed by my heirs while they live; and that such of the latter description as have no parents living, or if living are unable, or unwilling to provide for them, shall be bound by the Court until they shall arrive at the age of twenty-five years; and in cases where no record can be produced, whereby their ages can be ascertained, the judgment of the Court, upon its own view of the subject, shall be adequate and final. The Negroes thus bound, are (by their Masters or Mistresses) to be taught to read and write; and to be brought up to some useful occupation, agreeably to the laws of the Commonwealth of Virginia, providing for the support of orphan and other poor children.

"He has thought of everything, all the consequences. It is obvious he had been pondering this for along time," Lewis noted. He continued to read.

and I do hereby expressly forbid the sale, or transportation out of the said Commonwealth, of any slave I may die possessed of, under any pretense whatsoever. And I do moreover most pointedly, and most solemnly enjoin it upon my executors hereafter named, or the survivors of them, to see that this clause respecting slaves, and every part thereof be religiously fulfilled at the epoch at which it is directed to take place; without evasion, neglect, or delay, after the crops which may then be on the ground are harvested, particularly as it respects the aged and infirm; seeing that a regular and permanent fund be established for their support so long as there are subjects requiring it; not trusting to the uncertain provision to be made by individuals.

"Those are strong words," said Bushrod. "He does not want anyone to try to override his wishes and is giving us all important and specific directions."

"Just like his military directions," said George Steptoe, "clear and unquestionable."

"Sounds like this can't be turned around," thought Frank with a smile.

> *And to my mulatto man William (calling himself William Lee) I give immediate freedom; or if he should prefer it (on account of the accidents which have befallen him, and which have rendered him incapable of walking or of any active employment) to remain in the situation he now is, it shall be optional in him to do so: In either case, however, I allow him an annuity of thirty dollars during his natural life, which shall be independent of the victuals and clothes he has been accustomed to receive, if he chooses the last alternative; but in full, with his freedom, if he prefers the first; and this I give him as a testimony of my sense of his attachment to me, and for his faithful services during the Revolutionary War.*

Frank could contain himself no longer. His own brother was this very moment free. He smiled broadly and said so that all present could hear, "Thank you, Mr. President."

"I knew Billy during the war," said William Augustine. "He was right by the General's side, ready to do what was needed. Had many, many opportunities to go over to the redcoats with secrets, but he never did. Never. Huzzah for him."

"George often commented on how dependable and capable William was," Martha observed. "He held deep respect for him."

Frank stepped forward. "Excuse me, sir, but when will you tell him?"

"Do you think we can finish before dinner?" asked Martha. "Perhaps you could tell him then. You could ask him to come to the Mansion for something very important."

the aged and infirm;—seeing that a regular and permanent fund be established for their support so long as there are
subjects requiring it;—not trusting to
the uncertain provision to be made by
individuals.— And to my Mulatto
man William (calling himself William
Lee) I give immediate freedom; or if
he should prefer it (on account of the
accidents which have befallen him and
which have rendered him incapable of
walking or of any active employment)
to remain in the situation he now is,
it shall be optional in him to do so: In
either case however, I allow him an
annuity of thirty dollars during his
natural life, which shall be indepen-
dent of the victuals & cloaths he has
been accustomed to receive, if he chuses
the last alternative; but in full with his
his freedom, if he prefers the first; & this
I give him as a testimony of my sense
of his attachment to me, and for his
faithful services during the Revolutionary War.—

m. To the Trustees (Governors, or by whatsoever other name they may be designated)
of the Academy in the Town of Alexandria, I give and bequeath, in Trust,
four thousand dollars, or in other
words twenty of the shares which I

All agreed. Frank knew that time could not go fast enough for him to see his brother's face when he heard the news. He was trying, however, to appear calm.

"Gentlemen, we must proceed," said Lewis. "There is much more here. Could I have more tea, Frank? Let me see now. Oh, yes, here we are."

Item. To the Trustees (Governors, or by whatsoever other name they may be designated) of the Academy in the Town of Alexandria, I give and bequeath, in Trust, four thousand dollars, or in other words twenty of the shares which I hold in the Bank of Alexandria, towards the support of a Free school established at, and annexed to, the said Academy; for the purpose of Educating such Orphan children, or the children of such other poor and indigent persons as are unable to accomplish it with their own means; and who, in the judgment of the Trustees of the said Seminary, are best entitled to the benefit of this donation. The aforesaid twenty shares I give & bequeath in perpetuity; the dividends only of which are to be drawn for, and applied by the said Trustees for the time being, for the uses above mentioned; the stock to remain entire and untouched; unless indications of a failure of the said Bank should be so apparent, or a discontinuance thereof should render a removal of this fund necessary; in either of these cases, the amount of the Stock here devised, is to be vested in some other Bank or public Institution, whereby the interest may with regularity & certainty be drawn, and applied as above. And to prevent misconception, my meaning is, and is hereby declared to be, that these twenty shares are in lieu of, and not in addition to, the thousand pounds given by a missive letter some years ago; in consequence whereof an annuity of fifty pounds has since been paid towards the support of this Institution.

Item. Whereas by a Law of the Commonwealth of Virginia, enacted in the year 1785, the Legislature thereof was pleased (as an evidence of Its approbation of the services I had rendered the Public during the

George Washington

Revolution—and partly, I believe, in consideration of my having suggested
the vast advantages which the Community would derive from the extensions
of its Inland Navigation, under Legislative patronage) to present me with
one hundred shares of one hundred dollars each, in the incorporated company
established for the purpose of extending the navigation of James River from
tide water to the Mountains: and also with fifty shares of one hundred pounds
Sterling each, in the Corporation of another company, likewise established for
the similar purpose of opening the Navigation of the River Potomac from tide
water to Fort Cumberland, the acceptance of which, although the offer was
highly honourable, and grateful to my feelings, was refused, as inconsistent
with a principle which I had adopted, and had never departed from—
namely—not to receive pecuniary compensation for any services I could
render my country in its arduous struggle with great Britain, for its Rights;
and because I had evaded similar propositions from other States in the Union;
adding to this refusal, however, an intimation that, if it should be the pleasure
of the Legislature to permit me to appropriate the said shares to public uses,
I would receive them on those terms with due sensibility; and this it having
consented to, in flattering terms, as will appear by a subsequent Law, and
sundry resolutions, in the most ample and honourable manner, I proceed after
this recital, for the more correct understanding of the case, to declare—

"He was always insistent that he would not profit from his service, and now he directs that this gift from the state of Virginia be used for the public good. He could have just stowed the shares away. After all, they were given to him. He chose to turn them to public use," Bushrod observed.

"Sets an example for us all," said William Augustine.

Continuing on, Lewis read:

That as it has always been a source of serious regret with me, to see the youth of these United States sent to foreign Countries for the purpose of Education, often before their minds were formed, or they had imbibed any adequate ideas of the happiness of their own; contracting, too frequently, not only habits of dissipation & extravagance, but principles unfriendly to Republican Government and to the true & genuine liberties of Mankind; which, thereafter, are rarely overcome. For these reasons, it has been my ardent wish to see a plan devised on a liberal scale, which would have a tendency to spread systematic ideas through all parts of this rising Empire, thereby to do away local attachments and State prejudices, as far as the nature of things would, or indeed ought to admit, from our National Councils. Looking anxiously forward to the accomplishment of so desirable an object as this is (in my estimation) my mind has not been able to contemplate any plan more likely to effect the measure than the establishment of a UNIVERSITY in a central part of the United States, to which the youth of fortune and talents from all parts thereof might be sent for the completion of their Education in all the branches of polite literature; in arts and Sciences, in acquiring knowledge in the principles of Politics & good Government; and (as a matter of infinite Importance in my judgment) by associating with each other, and forming friendships in Juvenile years, be enabled to free themselves in a proper degree from those local prejudices & habitual jealousies which have just been mentioned; and which, when carried to excess, are never failing sources of disquietude to the Public mind, and pregnant of mischievous consequences to this Country: Under these impressions, so fully dilated,

Item. I give and bequeath in perpetuity the fifty shares which I hold in the Potomac Company (under the aforesaid Acts of the Legislature of Virginia) towards the endowment of a UNIVERSITY to be established within the limits of the District of Columbia, under the auspices of the General Government, if that government should incline to extend a fostering hand towards it; and until such Seminary is established, and the funds arising on

George Washington

these shares shall be required for its support, my further Will & desire is that
the profit accruing therefrom shall, whenever the dividends are made, be laid
out in purchasing Stock in the Bank of Columbia, or some other Bank, at
the discretion of my Executors; or by the Treasurer of the United States for
the time being under the direction of Congress; provided that Honourable
body should Patronize the measure, and the Dividends proceeding from the
purchase of such Stock is to be vested in more stock, and so on, until a sum
adequate to the accomplishment of the object is obtained, of which I have not
the smallest doubt, before many years passes away; even if no aid or encouraged
is given by Legislative authority, or from any other source.

Item. The hundred shares which I held in the James River Company,
I have given, and now confirm in perpetuity to, and for the use & benefit of
Liberty-Hall Academy, in the County of Rockbridge, in the Commonwealth
of Virginia.

"There it is," said George Steptoe. "Education. It was always a matter of much import for Uncle George. When my father died, he saw to it that Lawrence and I received education in Alexandria and then later at the College of Philadelphia. It does not surprise me that he has provided for a national university. Doesn't surprise me at all."

"Indeed," Martha said. "He spoke to me about it often."

"Seems there is more about your family, George," said Lewis. "You are specifically mentioned here."

Item. I release exonerate and discharge the Estate of my deceased brother
Samuel Washington from the payment of the money which is due to me
for the Land I sold to Philip Pendleton (lying in the County of Berkeley)
who assigned the same to him the said Samuel; who, by agreement was to
pay me therefor. And whereas by some contract (the purport of which was

William Lee 129

never communicated to me) between the said Samuel and his son Thornton Washington, the latter became possessed of the aforesaid Land, without any conveyance having passed from me, either to the said Pendleton, the said Samuel, or the said Thornton, and without any consideration having been made, by which neglect neither the legal nor equitable title has been alienated; it rests therefore with me to declare my intentions concerning the Premises—and these are, to give & bequeath the said land to whomsoever the said Thornton Washington (who is also dead) devised the same; or to his heirs forever if he died Intestate: Exonerating the estate of the said Thornton, equally with that of the said Samuel from payment of the purchase money; which, with Interest; agreeably to the original contract with the said Pendleton, would amount to more than a thousand pounds. And whereas two other Sons of my said deceased brother Samuel—namely, George Steptoe Washington and Lawrence Augustine Washington—were, by the decease of those to whose care they were committed, brought under my protection, and in consequence have occasioned advances on my part for their Education at College, and other Schools, for their board—clothing—and other incidental expenses, to the amount of near five thousand dollars over and above the Sums furnished by their Estate which Sum may be inconvenient for them, or their fathers Estate to refund. I do for these reasons acquit them, and the said estate, from the payment thereof. My intention being, that all accounts between them and me, and their father's estate and me shall stand balanced.

Silent tears rolled down George Steptoe's face as he thought of the many ways his uncle had provided for him over the years without ever speaking of his generosity or the debt owed. Now, even in death, he did not forget them.

"Lawrence, would you like me to read a bit and give you a rest?" asked Bushrod.

"That would be helpful," answered Lewis, "and Frank, I think the situation calls for a taste of that rum punch."

"Yes, sir, Mr. Lewis. It is ready right here," said Frank.

Lewis passed the document to Bushrod, who continued reading with the strong voice of a Supreme Court justice.

> *Item. The balance due to me from the Estate of Bartholomew Dandridge deceased (my wife's brother) and which amounted on the first day of October 1795 to four hundred and twenty five pounds (as will appear by an account rendered by his deceased son John Dandridge, who was the acting Executor of his father's Will) I release & acquit from the payment thereof. And the Negros (then thirty three in number) formerly belonging to the said estate, who were taken in execution—sold—and purchased in on my account in the year and ever since have remained in the possession, and to the use of Mary, Widow of the said Bartholomew Dandridge, with their increase, it is my Will & desire shall continue, & be in her possession, without paying hire, or making compensation for the same for the time past or to come, during her natural life; at the expiration of which, I direct that all of them who are forty years old & upwards, shall receive their freedom; all under that age and above sixteen, shall serve seven years and no longer; and all under sixteen years, shall serve until they are twenty-five years of age, and then be free. And to avoid disputes respecting the ages of any of these Negros, they are to be taken to the Court of the County in which they reside, and the judgment thereof, in this relation, shall be final; and a record thereof made; which may be adduced as evidence at any time thereafter, if disputes should arise concerning the same. And I further direct, that the heirs of the said Bartholomew Dandridge shall, equally, share the benefits arising from the services of the said Negros according to the tenor of this devise, upon the decease of their Mother.*

"He has not forgotten any slaves that he could legally claim," said Bushrod. "I am not surprised. And now let us see what else he has to say."

Item. If Charles Carter who intermarried with my niece Betty Lewis is not sufficiently secured in the title to the lots he had of me in the Town of Fredericksburg, it is my will & desire that my Executors shall make such conveyances of them as the Law requires, to render it perfect.

Item. To my Nephew William Augustine Washington and his heirs (if he should conceive them to be objects worth prosecuting) and to his heirs, a lot in the Town of Manchester (opposite to Richmond) No. 265—drawn on my sole account, and also the tenth of one or two, hundred acre lots, and two or three half acre lots in the City, and vicinity of Richmond, drawn in partnership with nine others, all in the lottery of the deceased William Byrd are given—as is also a lot which I purchased of John Hood, conveyed by William Willie and Samuel Gordon Trustees of the said John Hood, numbered 139 in the Town of Edinburgh, in the County of Prince George, State of Virginia.

"That is all very clear," said Bushrod. "No questions."

Item. To my Nephew Bushrod Washington, I give and bequeath all the Papers in my possession, which relate to my Civil and Military Administration of the affairs of this Country; I leave to him also, such of my private Papers as are worth preserving; and at the decease of wife, and before—if she is not inclined to retain them—I give and bequeath my library of Books and Pamphlets of every kind.

"What a gift," Bushrod blurted. "He was so meticulous with his papers. His thoughts and words are certainly a treasure, and I will protect them always. They are not just a gift to me but to the world." Taking a breath, he said, "I will continue now."

Item. Having sold Lands which I possessed in the State of Pennsylvania, and part of a tract held in equal right with George Clinton, late Governor of

George Washington

New York, in the State of New York; my share of land, & interest, in the Great Dismal Swamp, and a tract of land which I owned in the County of Gloucester; withholding the legal titles thereto, until the consideration money should be paid. And having moreover leased, & conditionally sold (as will appear by the tenor of the said leases) all my lands upon the Great Kanawha, and a tract upon Difficult Run, in the county of Loudoun, it is my Will and direction, that whensoever the Contracts are fully, & respectively complied with, according to the spirit; true intent & meaning thereof, on the part of the purchasers, their heirs or Assigns, that then, and in that case, Conveyances are to be made, agreeably to the terms of the said Contracts; and the money arising therefrom, when paid, to be vested in Bank stock; the dividends whereof, as of that also which is already vested therein, is to inure to my said Wife during her life—but the Stock itself is to remain, & be subject to the general distribution hereafter directed.

Item. To the Earl of Buchan I recommit "the box made of the Oak that sheltered the Great Sir William Wallace after the battle of Falkirk" presented to me by his Lordship, in terms too flattering for me to repeat, with a request "to pass it, on the event of my decease, to the man in my country, who should appear to merit it best, upon the same conditions that have induced him to send it to me." Whether easy, or not, to select the man who might comport with his Lordship's opinion in this respect, is not for me to say; but conceiving that no disposition of this valuable curiosity can be more eligible than the re-commitment of it to his own Cabinet, agreeably to the original design of the Goldsmiths Company of Edinburgh, who presented it to him, and at his request, consented that is should be transferred to me; I do give & bequeath the same to his Lordship, and in case of his decease, to his heir with my grateful thanks for the distinguished honour of presenting it to me; and more especially for the favourable sentiments with which he accompanied it.

Item. To my brother Charles Washington I give & bequeath the gold

William Lee 133

headed Cane left me by Doctor Franklin in his Will. I add nothing to it, because of the ample provision I have made for his Issue.

To the acquaintances and friends of my Juvenile years, Lawrence Washington & Robert Washington of Chotanck, I give my other two gold headed Canes, having my Arms engraved on them; and to each (as they will be useful where they live) I leave one of the Spy-glasses which constituted part of my equipage during the late War.

To my compatriot in arms, and old & intimate friend Doctor Craik, I give my Bureau (or as the Cabinet makers call it, Tambour Secretary) and the circular chair—an appendage of my Study.

To Doctor David Stuart I my large shaving Table and my Telescope.

To the Reverend, now Bryan, Lord Fairfax, I give a Bible in three large folio volumes, with notes, presented to me by the Right reverend Thomas Wilson, Bishop of Sodor & Man.

To General de la Fayette I give a pair of finely wrought steel Pistols, taken from the enemy in the Revolutionary War.

To my Sisters in law Hannah Washington & Mildred Washington; to my friends Eleanor Stuart, Hannah Washington of Fairfield, and Elizabeth Washington of Hayfield, I give, each, a mourning Ring of the value of one hundred dollars. These bequests are not made for the intrinsic value of them, but as mementos of my esteem & regard.

To Tobias Lear, I give the use of the Farm which he now holds, in virtue of a Lease from me to him and his deceased wife (for and during their natural lives) free from Rent, during his life; at the expiration of which, it is to be disposed as is hereinafter directed.

To Sally B. Haynie (a distant relation of mine) I give and bequeath three hundred dollars. To Sarah Green, daughter of the deceased Thomas Bishop, & to Ann Walker, daughter of John Alton, also deceased, I give, each, one hundred dollars, in consideration of the attachment of their fathers to me; each

George Washington

of whom having lived nearly forty years in my family.

To each of my Nephews, William Augustine Washington, George Lewis, George Steptoe Washington, Bushrod Washington and Samuel Washington, I give one of the Swords or Cutteaux of which I may die possessed; and they are to choose in the order they are named. These Swords are accompanied with an injunction not to unsheathe them for the purpose of shedding blood, except it be for self defense, or in defense of their Country and its rights; and in the latter case, to keep them unsheathed, and prefer falling with them in their hands, to the relinquishment thereof.

William Augustine rose from his chair and, punch in hand, and said, "Pistols, rings, swords, canes, Bibles, shaving tables—he has not forgotten a soul. And the instructions for us on the use of the sword, only to be used for the defense of the country and it rights and to not ever give it up—I will never forget these instructions."

"Never," the others echoed.

Martha looked at her pocket watch, rose and said, "We have been at this a long time. I think we should pause for a bit."

"Would this be a good time to tell William Lee of his freedom?" asked Bushrod.

"Yes, indeed," said Martha. "Frank, could you go and fetch him? Please don't tell him why he is being summoned. Let us enjoy his surprise."

"Yes, ma'am," said Frank. "Right away, right away." He almost skipped out of the room, flew out the back door, and ran down the muddy lane to the greenhouse barracks.

"William, William," he called as he came through the door.

"Yes, right here," said William as he looked up from his work table. "What has you so excited, brother?"

"I have been told to bring you to the Mansion."

William Lee

"Is something wrong? Is my work unsatisfactory?"

"No and no; just come with me quickly," said Frank.

"All right, all right. I need to at least wash my face. Haven't done that yet today."

"Yes, but be quick about it."

As William washed his face, he quickly went over in his mind what the matter could be. He was especially concerned because his friend and protector was no longer there to speak for him.

He found his tattered greatcoat and slowly put it on.

"This is no time to saunter," said Frank. "They are waiting for you."

"Who is 'they'?" asked William.

"You'll see."

William found his crutches and Frank helped him navigate the accumulated slush as they made their way to the Mansion.

Upon entering the room William recognized most of the men gathered there. He had known them during the Revolution. They were happy to see him again and smiled as he entered.

Bushrod came forward and shook William's hand, an unusual courtesy toward a slave. "William," he said, "we are gathered here as executors of the General's will and we have come to a point where he mentions you."

William still was not sure whether this was a good or bad thing, and as a slave he had learned not to show his emotions and not to question.

"Would you like to hear what General Washington said about you?'

"Yes, sir," answered William softly with eyes lowered.

"Let me see," said Bushrod as he searched for the right section.

"Yes, here it is." He smiled as he read.

> And to my mulatto man William (calling himself William Lee) I give immediate freedom; or if he should prefer it (on account of the accidents which have befallen him, and which have rendered him incapable of walking or of any active employment) to remain in the situation he now is, it shall be optional in him to do so: In either case, however, I allow him an annuity of thirty dollars during his natural life, which shall be independent of the victuals and clothes he has been accustomed to receive, if he chooses the last alternative; but in full, with his freedom, if he prefers the first; and this I give him as a testimony of my sense of his attachment to me, and for his faithful services during the Revolutionary War.

All in the room clapped and smiled. Frank grinned from ear to ear.

"Immediate freedom," thought William. "Could you read that again, sir?" he asked softly.

"Of course," said Bushrod.

When the second reading was finished, William leaned heavily on his crutches and said, "I find I have to sit down, sir. A free man. A free man," he repeated and slumped into the nearest chair, trying to believe what he had just heard.

"Yes, William, as of this moment you are free," said Bushrod. "Looks to me that you could use a taste of Mount Vernon's punch. Frank, can you do that for us?"

Frank gave a cup of punch to all present including William. "This calls for a toast," said Bushrod. "To William and the many free years he has ahead."

"Hear, hear," the men chorused and lifted their cups. "To William!"

"Thank you," said William quietly as he began to absorb the news of a free future. He looked at Frank as if to say, "How about you?" Frank smiled and indicated that they would speak later.

"William, I am very happy for you. My husband often spoke to me of your ability and your loyalty. And now he has rewarded you even in death," said Martha. And then, turning to her nephews, she said, "Dinner is served in the Dinning Room."

William knew that, free or not, this invitation did not include him. He thanked everyone as they made their way to the table and then he headed for the barracks, his head spinning.

The Dinning Room was bathed in the brightness of a clear winter light as the executors took their places. They were still full of the joy of watching William as the news of his freedom was read to him. They took their places smiling.

Frank and his team of other enslaved servants passed oyster ragout (Martha's favorite), chicken fricassee, barbecued pork, salads, applesauce, biscuits, and for dessert, pound cake and chocolate puffs, accompanied by the General's favorite Madeira.

Table talk centered on the will and the consequences that might follow.

Taking a sip of wine, George Steptoe turned to Bushrod and said, "He left you all his papers. That is quite a gift and quite a responsibility."

"I agree on both counts," said Bushrod. "He was methodical and precise with all his papers. He leaves us all much about the founding of this country and the military battles that he waged. And his notes on Mount Vernon are detailed and practical. They will be a big help."

"I am a bit concerned about his giving his slaves freedom," said

William Augustine. "That will have repercussions for many—for slaves, slaveholders, slave sellers. I am not sure where it will lead us. The Virginia slaveholders will be worried. In fact, all of us at this table are slaveholders. What will it mean for us?"

"He often said to me that slavery is the one thing that could divide the country," said Lawrence. "I can't say I disagree."

Martha listened to the conversation closely. She turned to the group and said slowly, "This has put me in a delicate position. I cannot free my slaves. They belong to the Custis estate. And what happens to people like Lucy and Frank? I can't free Lucy, my slave, but Frank, because he is George's slave, will be freed. But they are married. What will happen? And what about their children?"

Everyone at the table felt uncomfortable. They did not have advice that would fix the problem and did not know what to tell their aunt that would give her some kind of peace.

"We will be here to help," said Bushrod. "Don't worry, now. I will be here."

Martha heard their words but they did not relive her anxiety.

Taking their tea, the group returned to the Front Parlor and resumed their places to finish hearing the will. Frank provided more punch and offered pipes to those who smoked tobacco.

"Well, now," said Bushrod. "That was a lovely meal, Aunt Martha, and it gives us strength to get back to our purpose. Where were we? Yes, here it is."

And now
Having gone through these specific devises, with explanations for the more correct understanding of the meaning and design of them; I proceed to the distribution of the more important parts of my Estate, in manner following—
First To my Nephew Bushrod Washington and his heirs (partly in

William Lee   139

consideration of an intimation to his deceased father while we were Bachelors,
& he had kindly undertaken to superintend my Estate during my Military
Services in the former War between Great Britain & France, that if I should
fall therein, Mount Vernon (then less extensive in domain than at present)
should become his property) I give and bequeath all that part thereof which
is comprehended within the following limits—viz.—Beginning at the ford
of Houndue Run, near my Mill, and extending along the road, and bounded
thereby as it now goes, & ever has gone since my recollection of it, to the ford of
little hunting Creek at the Gum spring until it comes to a knoll, opposite to an
old road which formerly passed through the lower field of Muddy Hole Farm;
at which, on the north side of the said road are three red, or Spanish, Oaks
marked as a corner, and a stone placed. Thence by a line of trees to be marked,
rectangular to the back line, or outer boundary of the tract between Thomson
Mason & myself. Thence with that line Easterly (now double ditching with
a Post & Rail fence thereon) to the run of little hunting Creek. Thence with
that run which is the boundary between the Lands of the late Humphrey
Peake and me, to the tide water of the said Creek; thence by that water to
Potomac River. Thence with the River to the mouth of Houndue Creek. And
thence with the said Houndue Creek to the place of beginning at the aforesaid
ford; containing upwards of four thousand Acres, be the same more or less—
together with the Mansion house and all other buildings and improvements
thereon.

Bushrod coughed lightly and shifted in his chair. He was not surprised—perhaps a bit embarrassed. The others were not surprised either. They knew there had always a special closeness between the families and the General was recognizing that.

"It is another honor," said Bushrod. "It also comes with much responsibility. I hope I can meet his my uncle's trust."

He resumed reading.

George Washington

Second In consideration of the consanguinity between them and my wife, being as nearly related to her as to myself, as on account of the affection I had for, and the obligation I was under to, their father when living, who from his youth had attached himself to my person, and followed my fortunes through the vicissitudes of the late Revolution—afterwards devoting his time to the Superintendence of my private concerns for many years, whilst my public employments rendered it impracticable for me to do it myself, thereby affording me essential Services, and always performing them in a manner the most filial and respectful—for these reasons I say, I give and bequeath to George Fayette Washington, and Lawrence [Charles] Augustine Washington and their heirs, my Estate East of little hunting Creek, lying on the River Potomac; including the Farm of 360 Acres, Leased to Tobias Lear as noticed before, and containing in the whole, by Deeds, Two thousand and Seventy seven acres—be it more or less. Which said Estate it is my Will & desire should be equitably, & advantageously divided between them, according to quantity, quality & other circumstances when the youngest shall have arrived at the age of twenty one years, by three judicious and disinterested men; one to be chosen by each of the brothers, and the third by these two. In the meantime, if the termination of my wife's interest therein should have ceased, the profits arising therefrom are to be applied for their joint uses and benefit.

Third And whereas it has always been my intention, since my expectation of having Issue has ceased, to consider the Grandchildren of my wife in the same light as I do my own relations, and to act a friendly part by them; more especially by the two whom we have reared from their earliest infancy—namely—Eleanor Parke Custis, & George Washington Parke Custis. And whereas the former of these hath lately intermarried with Lawrence Lewis, a son of my deceased Sister Betty Lewis, by which union the inducement to provide for them both has been increased; Wherefore, I give & bequeath to the said Lawrence Lewis & Eleanor Parke Lewis, his wife,

William Lee 141

and their heirs, the residue of my Mount Vernon Estate, not already devised to my Nephew Bushrod Washington; comprehended within the following description—viz.—All the land North of the Road leading from the ford of Houndue Run to the Gum spring as described in the devise of the other part of the tract, to Bushrod Washington, until it comes to the Stone & three red or Spanish Oaks on the knoll. Thence with the rectangular line to the back line (between Mr. Mason & me)—thence with that line westerly, along the new double ditch to Houndue Run, by the tumbling Dam of my Mill; thence with the said run to the ford aforementioned; to which I add all the Land I possess West of the said Houndue Run, & Houndue Creek—bounded Easterly & Southerly thereby; together with the Mill, Distillery, and all other houses & improvements on the premises, making together about two thousand Acres— be it more or less.

Lewis smiled and said, "This is a delight. Nelly will be so happy to know that we now own so much of what is dear to her and her childhood memories. Her grandpapa meant a great deal to her. I suppose this makes us neighbors, Bushrod!"

"Absolutely," said Bushrod. "This may be a big task, and I am happy to share that responsibility, Lawrence."

Fourth Actuated by the principal already mentioned, I give and bequeath to George Washington Parke Custis, the Grandson of my wife, and my Ward, and to his heirs, the tract I hold on four mile run in the vicinity of Alexandria, containing one thousand two hundred acres, more or less, & my entire Square, number twenty one, in the City of Washington.

"It is amazing to me how clear and precise he is about everything. He put many hours of effort into this," said Samuel.
"And there is more. He did not forget anyone," said Bushrod.

In witness of all, and of
each of the things herein-
contained, I have set my
hand and seal, this ninth
day of July, in the year
One thousand seven hun=
dred and ninety and of
the Independence of the
United States the twenty
fourth.—

G. Washington

Fifth All the rest and residue of my Estate, real & personal—not disposed of in manner aforesaid—In whatsoever consisting—wheresoever lying—and whensoever found—a schedule of which, as far as is recollected, with a reasonable estimate of its value, is hereunto annexed—I desire may be sold by my Executors at such times—in such manner—and on such credits (if an equal, valid, and satisfactory distribution of the specific property cannot be made without) as, in their judgment shall be most conducive to the interest of the parties concerned; and the monies arising therefrom to be divided into twenty three equal parts, and applied as follow—viz.

To William Augustine Washington, Elizabeth Spotswood, Jane Thornton, and the heirs of Ann Ashton; son, and daughters of my deceased brother Augustine Washington, I give and bequeath four parts; that is—one part to each of them.

To Fielding Lewis, George Lewis, Robert Lewis, Howell Lewis & Betty Carter, sons and daughter of my deceased Sister Betty Lewis, I give & bequeath five other parts—one to each of them.

To George Steptoe Washington, Lawrence Augustine Washington, Harriot Parks, and the heirs of Thornton Washington, sons & daughter of my deceased brother Samuel Washington, I give and bequeath other four parts, one part to each of them.

To Corbin Washington, and the heirs of Jane Washington, Son & daughter of my deceased brother John Augustine Washington, I give & bequeath two parts; one part to each of them.

To Samuel Washington, Francis Ball & Mildred Hammond, son & daughters of my Brother Charles Washington, I give & bequeath three parts; one part to each of them. And to George Fayette Washington, Charles Augustine Washington & Maria Washington, sons and daughter of my deceased Nephew George Augustine Washington, I give one other part; that is—to each a third of that part.

George Washington

To Elizabeth Parke Law, Martha Parke Peter, and Eleanor Parke Lewis, I give and bequeath three other parts, that is a part to each of them.

And to my Nephews Bushrod Washington & Lawrence Lewis, and to my ward, the grandson of My wife, I give and bequeath one other part; that is, a third thereof to each of them. And if it should so happen, that any of the persons whose names are here enumerated (unknown to me) should now be deceased, or should die before me, that in either of these cases, the heirs of such deceased person shall, notwithstanding, derive all the benefits of the bequest; in the same manner as if he, or she, was actually living at the time.

"Seems he has divided everything up in a fair and useful manner, and forgotten no one." said William Augustine. "Isn't that just like him? What an uncle to have."

"And now he needs to add a bit of advice about the Potomac Company. That was his special interest," said Bushrod. "Here it is."

And by way of advice, I recommend it to my Executors not to be precipitate in disposing of the landed property (herein directed to be sold) if from temporary causes the Sale thereof should be dull; experience having fully evinced, that the price of land (especially above the Falls of the Rivers, & on the Western Waters) has been progressively rising, and cannot be long checked in its increasing value. And I particularly recommend it to such of the Legatees (under this clause of my Will) as can make it convenient, to take each a share of my Stock in the Potomac Company in preference to the amount of what it might sell for; being thoroughly convinced myself, that no uses to which the money can be applied will be so productive as the Tolls arising from this navigation when in full operation (and this from the nature of things it must be 'ere long) and more especially if that of the Shenandoah is added thereto.

The family Vault at Mount Vernon requiring repairs, and being improperly situated besides, I desire that a new one of Brick, and upon a larger Scale, may be built at the foot of what is commonly called the Vineyard Inclosure, on the ground which is marked out. My remains, with those of my deceased relatives (now in the old Vault) and such others of my family as may chose to be entombed there, may be deposited. And it is my express desire that my Corpse may be Interred in a private manner, without parade, or funeral Oration.

"Well, that did not happen, did it?" said Bushrod, looking at his fellow executors. "There was a parade and orations indeed."

"Don't think that could have been helped," replied Lewis. "There were so many people who wanted to honor him and they would not take no for an answer. They all felt he deserved it."

"Well, here, is the last bit where he names us as executors," said Bushrod.

Lastly I constitute and appoint my dearly beloved wife Martha Washington, My Nephews William Augustine Washington, Bushrod Washington, George Steptoe Washington, Samuel Washington, & Lawrence Lewis, & my ward George Washington Parke Custis (when he shall have arrived at the age of twenty years) Executrix & Executors of this Will & testament,

In the construction of which it will readily be perceived that no professional character has been consulted, or has had any Agency in the draught—and that, although it has occupied many of my leisure hours to digest, & to through it into its present form, it may, notwithstanding, appear crude and incorrect. But having endeavoured to be plain, and explicit in all Devises—even at the expense of prolixity, perhaps of tautology, I hope, and trust, that no disputes will arise concerning them; but if, contrary to expectation, the case should be otherwise from the want of legal expression, or the usual technical terms,

George Washington

or because too much or too little has been said on any of the Devises to be consonant with law, My Will and direction expressly is, that all disputes (if unhappily any should arise) shall be decided by three impartial and intelligent men, known for their probity and good understanding; two to be chosen by the disputants—each having the choice of one—and the third by those two. Which three men thus chosen, shall, unfettered by Law, or legal constructions, declare their sense of the Testators intention; and such decision is, to all intents and purposes to be as binding on the Parties as if it had been given in the Supreme Court of the United States.

"The Supreme Court of the United States," said Lewis. "He put great faith in that."

"And I strongly desire that we will fulfill that faith," said Bushrod.

In witness of all, and of each of the things herein contained, I have set my hand and Seal, this ninth day of July, in the year One thousand seven hundred and ninety-nine and of the Independence of the United States the twenty-fourth.

"My goodness, he not only gives a time from the birth of Jesus Christ but from the birth of the nation," said George Steptoe.

"I suspect that is all," said Samuel.

"Yes, that is it," said Bushrod.

A heavy silence fell as all present realized these were the last words from their uncle and they were responsible for seeing his wishes carried out. These were meaningful words for the family and for the nation.

Martha was exceptionally quiet, thinking of her words at the deathbed: " 'Tis well. All is now over; I shall soon follow him. I have no more trials to pass through."

William Lee

"It occurs to me," said George Steptoe, "that since Lawrence lives right here at Mount Vernon and Bushrod nearby, perhaps you could handle what still needs to be done with this will and oversee that its directions are carried out. The rest of us are further away. We, of course, would be happy to help when called upon."

"Sounds reasonable," said Lewis. "I will file the will with probate at the Fairfax Courthouse as soon as possible. And Bushrod and I will keep you informed and give advice and counsel to Aunt Martha."

"I want you all to stay the night with us here," said Martha. "It is getting dark and there is no reason for you to leave yet."

The cousins happily accepted the invitation, pleased at the chance to spend a bit more time with each other.

The next morning as winter dawn swept over Mount Vernon, they breakfasted and then Peter brought their carriages and horses from the stables, cleaned and ready to take them home. They said their farewells to their aunt and left, each wealthier than when they came, not just in valuables but in the discovery that their uncle's will would make a difference for the fledgling country and its dependence on slavery. That their uncle was indeed a man of principal and compassion.

Chapter Eighteen

AFTERMATH

Monday
December 30, 1799
8 p.m.

When William left the Mansion that afternoon, he walked out a free man, still slightly in a state of shock. As he opened the barracks door his newfound life was beginning to take on reality. A fast rush of joy consumed him and seeped through his mind, bubbling into his soul. He sat now by the fire in his tattered greatcoat. He had decided to sleep there this night. He would not go to the enslaved men's barracks. "I am slave no more," he said to himself. "I do not belong there. Yes, I am slave no more! No more! Hallelujah!"

Soon Frank appeared, having finished his duties in the Mansion. He too was full of joy and they embraced with brotherly love. Through their many years of enslavement they had been there for each other in good times and bad, and now this was a good time.

"You are free right now, brother. Right now. Right now."

"But what about you? Didn't the General free you too?" William asked.

"Well," said Frank, "that will only happen when the mistress dies. That is what the will says. I heard them read it. After the mistress dies, the rest of the General's slaves are to be freed."

"And who knows when that will happen?" said William.

"Who knows?" said Frank. "But at least the future carries hope. I am not sure how to tell Lucy," he added.

"Why? Won't she be freed with you?"

"No, she is a Custis slave. You see, when the General married the mistress, she was the widow of Daniel Custis, a big man with big money. But he died without a will. So according to the Virginia law, his slaves are hers until she dies, and then they go to the Custis estate, grandchildren, cousins and nephews. They will all be divided up, wives, husbands, children."

"So for the Custis slaves there will be no freedom?"

"That's right," said Frank, drawing a chair up to the fire.

"Once I overheard the General say, not too long ago, that there are a hundred and fifty-three Custis slaves. Folks like you and me."

"Frank, I have a bit of whiskey from the General's distillery. He gave it to me not long ago but he insisted I keep it a secret. Would you like a taste now?"

"Just a taste," said Frank. "I would be in big trouble if they found out."

William hobbled to his worktable, pulled the bottle from under a mound of leather, and handed it to his brother.

"So if you were free, maybe you could buy Lucy when the mistress dies."

"I suppose—but where would I find the money? And what will you do, William? Will you leave Mount Vernon?"

"I don't know. I haven't had time to think about it. But the will did say I would be getting regular money. Just think, regular money and a free man. Frank I had great respect for the General, and he returned it."

"I must go to Lucy now," said Frank. "She will be anxious to hear everything." As the light was slowly dying and a clear sky displayed the endless quiet stars, Frank put his arm around William, then left the cobbler's shop, carrying the message to his wife that sometime in the future he would be a free man but she and the children would still be enslaved.

William took another sip of whiskey began to plan his life as a free man. Within a few minutes his thoughts were interrupted when the door opened, bringing in a blast of cold air and Christopher Sheels.

"I just heard, William. You are free man. Glory to God. You are free. Just like you told me it could happen. It happened to you, my good man."

"Yes," said William. "It did indeed."

"But it can't happen for me, not for me. I am a Custis slave, and when the mistress dies I will go to one of her grandchildren and be enslaved there. Oh God, William. I can't. I can't," he said, tears flowing down his face.

"Now, Christopher, don't give up. I never thought I would be free, but I am. You have to have faith that you will overcome. You are still young and much can happen in a young life. You have to hold on to your soul, young man. Hold on. Hold on. Here, take a sip of my whiskey—celebrate with me."

"I can do that," said Christopher, "but I can never get rid of this burden of slavery."

"You don't have a choice right now," said William. "But you

must believe that things can change. You must. My mama always said, They can take your body but they can't take your soul. Don't let them take your soul, Christopher."

Christopher took a deep breath and tried to accept that the future could be better. Past experience, however, did not give him hope.

William clapped Christopher's shoulder and said, "I will be here for you. For now, try not to keep thinking about the future. Live for today."

Christopher tried to smile, but his thoughts were in other places. He shook William's outstretched hand and went out into the darkness.

Chapter 19

PLOTS, FEARS, AND EARLY FREEDOM

Spring 1800
Mount Vernon

During the weeks that followed, the news of imminent freedom for some and continued enslavement for others spread quickly through Mount Vernon.

Martha, accustomed to giving orders and having them followed promptly, sensed that things were different for the slaves held by George, those who would be freed at her death. She felt they did not respond to orders quite as quickly; they walked with their head up and seemed less afraid of her presence. She had heard that there was celebrating in some of the quarters.

One afternoon she spoke with Lawrence Lewis about her concerns.

"Why wouldn't they want me to die sooner rather than later? It is to their benefit to see me go. In fact, one of the overseers tells me he found a few slaves making plans to leave right now, but he

William Lee   153

was able to put a stop to it. Or maybe they might even try to kill me."

"Aunt Martha, don't let your thoughts carry you that far. Uncle George never had fears that would happen, and besides, his slaves are beholden to him and would not do that, ever."

"Sometimes I get the feeling they might, especially when I see them whispering to each other."

"I am here," said Lawrence. "I will keep watch."

As weeks passed, Martha's fears did not subside but actually increased. She asked Bushrod Washington and a good friend of his, future Chief Justice John Marshall, to come to Mount Vernon to talk.

"Aunt Martha," said Bushrod, "Lawrence has told me of your fears, and seeing how they are continually with you, I think you should be quit of Uncle George's slaves now. It is the only thing that will give you peace. Free them all now."

"Can I do that?"

"Of course you can," said Marshall, "and I agree with Bushrod that it should be done now rather than later. I will draw up the papers and you will sign them and they will be freed by January 1, 1801. And it will be over. I will see to it that it is done quickly and easily. You will not have to worry."

"If it is that easy, we should by all means do it. I would feel much better, and I know George would agree with the plan. Maybe tonight I will sleep without thinking about fire or poison. Oh, Bushrod, I miss him so."

Bushrod put his arms around her. "He was a great man, Aunt Martha, and you were always there for him. Thank you for that."

She smiled gave him a hug and said, "You are busy with many

important things. Go now. Thank you for coming."

As she watched the carriage proceed down the drive, she tried once again to suppress her constant grief. In the months since her husband's death she had not once entered their bedroom or his study. She mentioned often that she thought her own death was not far off and in some ways longed for it to happen so she could join her husband.

156 *George Washington*

Chapter 20
FREE AT LAST

After the first of January 1801, things changed dramatically at Mount Vernon. George Washington's 123 slaves were freed. There was celebration on the farms and in the Mansion, but joy was tempered by uncertainty about what to do next. Some decided to stay on at Mount Vernon as hired help; some left to find work in the surrounding area. Within a few years, some were even able to buy land. Those the General had provided for because of their old age or their young age stayed on and received the benefits that his will called for.

William Lee decided to remain. He continued his work as a cobbler. Visitors to Mount Vernon made a point of meeting him, asking him questions about the war and his good friend, General Washington. He was a legendary raconteur and enjoyed speaking with the visitors. He died at Mount Vernon around 1810. He is believed to be buried in Mount Vernon's slave cemetery.

It appears that Frank Lee lived as a free man in the vicinity of Mount Vernon, close to his enslaved family at Woodlawn, the home of Nelly and Lawrence Lewis. There is no record that he was able to buy his wife and three children, Philip, Mike, and Patty, from them. At seventeen Philip was sent as a slave to live with another grandchild of Martha's, Nelly's brother, George Washington Parke Custis. The grounds of his estate, Arlington House, became Arlington National Cemetery.

This situation of some free and some not free created uncertainty and confusion. The plantation itself was struggling in the absence of the disciplined and organized General. Martha still remained the hospitable and welcoming hostess, but she could not hide her continuing grief. In the spring of 1802 she became ill with what was called bilious fever and died May 22 at the age of seventy-one. She was a woman of her time: wife, mother, plantation manager, family linchpin; brave, unflinching supporter of her husband and the new country he helped establish, gracious hostess and true friend. She was placed next to her "old man" in the family vault.

Martha's death brought with it all that her Custis slaves had feared. Since her first husband had died without a will, her slaves could not, by Virginia law, be inherited by her second husband's family. This meant they would leave Mount Vernon and go to the homes of four Custis relatives. It was what so many had dreaded.

Christopher Sheels was sent to Arlington House. His experience at Mount Vernon as carpenter, house servant, and valet made him highly valuable. It is not known whether he ever attained freedom. His new master, George Washington Parke Custis, like his step grandfather, did free his slaves in his will. Custis died in 1857. At that time Christopher would have been about eighty-two; he probably did not live to see freedom.

George Washington Parke Custis also inherited Caroline

and Peter Hardiman. Caroline had been George and Martha's chambermaid and was called upon to provide services of all kinds at Mount Vernon. She was an excellent seamstress, cared for Nelly's baby, and was at the General's bedside when he died. Her husband, Peter, highly skilled with horses, was in charge of the stables.

Caroline and Peter had eight children. All were inherited by George Washington Parke Custis. This step grandson of the General undoubtedly was very familiar with this family, as he was reared at Mount Vernon from the age of six months. Records indicate that four of them attained freedom. It is not clear whether the others were ever emancipated.

Davy and Molly Gray were also dower slaves and were inherited by Nelly and Lawrence Lewis.

Slavery, along with all the horrors and cruelty that the system demands, would continue in the United States for the next sixty-three years. Slaves were bought, sold, and unpaid for their labor. Families were torn apart. As President Washington had predicted, "Nothing but the rooting out of slavery can perpetuate the existence of our union, by consolidating it in a common bond of principle." The Civil War brought about "the rooting out" which culminated in the 13th Amendment, eliminating slavery in the United States. The evils and consequences that the system created are deep, and their effects remain with us still. With us still also is the compassion of George Washington and many of our ancestors who stood for the African American because it was the right thing to do. By persistence, courage, cooperation, and determination, African Americans have led the way to become part of the legacy that defines America.

George Washington Genealogy

Jane Butler		Augustine Washington		Mary Ball
(1699–1728)		(1694–1743)		(1708–1789)
m. 1715				m. 1731

Lawrence Washington (1718–1752) m. Ann Fairfax (?–1761)	Augustine Washington (1720–1762) m. Ann Aylett	Betty Washington (1733–1797) m. Fielding Lewis (1725–1781)	George Washington (1732–1799) m. Martha Dandridge (1731–1802)

Samuel Washington (1734–1781) m. Jane Champ Mildred Thornton Louisa Chapman Ann Steptoe Susannah Perrin	John Augustine Washington (1736–1787) m. Hannah Bushrod	Charles Washington (1738–1799) m. Mildred Thornton

William Lee Genealogy

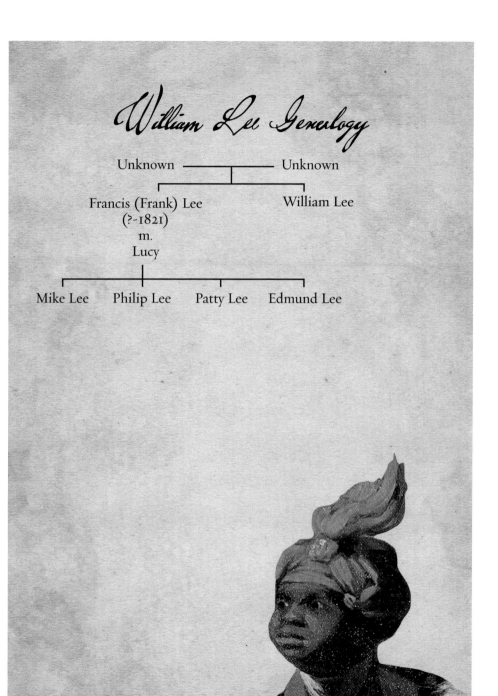

Unknown ———————— Unknown

Francis (Frank) Lee   William Lee
(?-1821)
m.
Lucy

Mike Lee   Philip Lee   Patty Lee   Edmund Lee

George Washington

ILLUSTRATION CREDITS

The cover for *By His Side* is a detail from John Trumbull's (1780) portrait of George Washington. The man by Washington's side is probably meant to represent William Lee, Washington's enslaved valet. Trumbull painted the picture while studying in London and portrayed William Lee wearing a turban. Artists at that time often used turbans to portray enslaved servants, an attempt to make them look exotic. William Lee probably never wore such headgear.

William Lee

BIBLIOGRAPHY

Botume, Elizabeth Hyde. First Days Amongst the Contrabands. Lee and Shepard, 1892.

Brighton, Ray. The Checkered Career of Tobias Lear. Portsmouth, NH, 1985.

Cadou, Carol Borchert., Nancy Carter. Crump, and Stephen A. McLeod. Dining with the Washingtons: Historic Recipes, Entertainment, and Hospitality from Mount Vernon. Mount Vernon, VA: Mount Vernon Ladies Association, 2011.

Chernow, Ron. Washington - a Life. Penguin Books Ltd, 2011.

Connell, Janice T. The Spiritual Journey of George Washington. North Charleston, SC: Create Space, 2013.

Flexner, James Thomas. Washington: the Indispensable Man. Boston: Little, Brown and Company, 1974.

Fraser, Flora. The Washingtons: "Join'd by Friendship, Crown'd by Love". New York: Alfred A. Knopf, 2015.

Freeman, Douglas Southall. George Washington: Planter and Patriot. Vol. 3. Scribners, 1951.

Graham, Winston. Poldark: Ross Poldark. Naperville, IL: Sourcebooks Inc., 2015.

Henriques, Peter R. The Death of George Washington: He Died as He Lived. Mount Vernon, VA: Mount Vernon Ladies Association, 2000.

President Washington's Diaries from 1791 to 1799. Big Byte Books, 2016.

Jensen, Oliver. The American Heritage Cookbook: and Illustrated History of American Eating and Drinking. New York: American Heritage, 1964.

MacLeod, Jessie, Mary V. Thompson, and Susan Prendergast Schoelwer.

Lives Bound Together: Slavery at George Washington's Mount Vernon. Mount Vernon, VA: Mount Vernon Ladies Association, 2016.

McClafferty, Carla Killough. Buried Lives: the Enslaved People of George Washington's Mount Vernon. New York: Holiday House, 2018.

Mount Vernon Ladies' Association. George Washington's Mount Vernon Official Guidebook, n.d.

Philbrick, Nathaniel. In the Hurricanes Eye: the Genius of George Washington and the Victory at Yorktown. NY, NY: Viking, 2018.

Rhodehamel, John. George Washington: the Wonder of the Age, n.d.

Saxton, Martha. The Widow Washington: the Life of Mary Washington. New York: Farrar, Straus and Giroux, 2019.

Smucker, Philip G. Riding with George Sportsmanship & Chivalry in the Making of Americas First President. Chicago: Chicago Review Press, 2017.

Thompson, Mary V. In the Hands of a Good Providence: Religion in the Life of George Washington and His Family. Charlottesville: University of Virginia Press, 2008.

Thompson, Mary V. "The Only Unavoidable Subject of Regret": George Washington, Slavery, and the Enslaved Community at Mount Vernon. Charlottesville: University of Virginia Press, 2019.

Washington, George, and Carolyn P. Yoder. George Washington, the Writer: a Treasury of Letters, Diaries, and Public Documents. Honesdale, PA: Boyds Mills Press, 2003.

Wiencek, Henry. An Imperfect God: George Washington, His Slaves, and the Creation of America. New York: Farrar, Straus and Giroux, 2004.

"George Washington's Last Will and Testament, 9 July 1799,

Founder's Online, National Archives, accessed April 11, 2019.

https://founders.archieves.gov/documents/

Washington/06-04-02-0404-0001. (Original source: The Papers of

George Washington,

Retirement series, vol.4, 20 April 1799-13 December 1799, ed. W.W.

Abbot. Charlottesville: University Press of Virginia, 1999, pp. 478-511.)

William Lee   167

AUTHOR'S NOTE

Many people often ask what is real and what is fiction in a historical novel. Most of the events described in this one, such as Yorktown, crossing the Delaware, and the snowball fight did take place.

We are blessed with an immense amount of information about George Washington, his family, and his associates. The words of many of them have been recorded and saved for posterity. Of course, a novelist must create dialogue. Tobias Lear recorded George Washington's death. The scene and dialogue reflect this record. There are many different diagnoses of what was caused his death. Some medical experts say epiglottis, an extreme infection in the throat, was the cause. Others say it was pneumonia or an abscess.

There is agreement that removing forty percent of his blood did not help and probably hastened his death.

Washington did have a hound called Sweetlips. The slaves in the story—William Lee, Frank and Lucy Lee, Caroline and Peter Hardiman, Christopher Sheels, Davy and Molly Gray—all lived on the Mount Vernon plantation during the time of the story.

For someone living in the twenty-first century to attempt to write about the lives of the enslaved living in the eighteenth century is a tremendous challenge. To attempt to look into their hearts, minds, and souls is a sacred journey that demands the utmost respect. Because most enslaved people were denied the right to read and write, few records exist of their feelings, words, and actions. Their dialogue, activities, and thoughts had to be created. For this reason we call it historical fiction. My hope is that this work will help us all take a step closer to understanding slavery and the scars the system left on our country.

William Lee